That Church Life

Teresa B. Howell

Independent

Self-Published through Walking In Victory Int. L.L.C

P.O. Box 15171

Durham, NC 27704

Printed in the USA

THAT CHURCH LIFE

SPECIAL DEDICATION

This book is dedicated to my Grandmother, Era B. Ellis, and my mother, Helen J. Ellis, who both were the apple of my eye. I miss and love you both, R.I.P.

Teresa B. Howell

ACKNOWLEDGMENTS

I would like to thank God Almighty for giving me the strength to finish this book despite setbacks. I also want to thank my very supportive and dedicated husband, Calvin Howell III, who pushed me through this process to ensure that I gave my very best. I'm thankful for my boys for cheering me on and reading sample chapters along the way. Joshua, Dray and Calvin James are my biggest supporters.

I would not be complete if I didn't thank my mother-in-law, Rose C. Howell who encouraged me to start the writing progress during a difficult time in my life. I discovered talent that I didn't know existed from her push.

Thankful for my parents, Helen J. Ellis and James M. Ellis, who supported me 120% in any and everything I set my mind to. Aunt Janice "Elaine" Woods and Aunt Michelle Kallie, my backbone: THANK YOU!

THAT CHURCH LIFE

Chapter 1

"Lord, forgive my sin!" echoed down Burlington Street and off the row of brick tenements. I ran back and forth, screaming the words at the top of my lungs with a preacher's tone.

Is this happening to me? Is this a dream? Help, please!

My feet were red and bruised. *Where are my shoes? Why isn't anyone helping me? Do they not hear me screaming?* I felt my eyes fluttering as I looked up at the horizon. I was not surprised to see window shades pulled up and people glaring from their homes. All those empty stares watching me for a story, but not to help me.

I stood in the middle of the street feeling insecure and paranoid while dabbing at burning ears. My anxiety got the best of me. Tinges of red on the edges of my fingertips confirmed all my fears.

Blood! But how? Where? I need to find someplace to hide!

Numb and still very confused, my chanting for help became louder. "Lord, my God! Help me, Lord!"

My screams and cries did not cease. "Lord, please forgive me for my sin."

The scene of violence was stuck in my head. *Hey man. Don't shoot!* I could still hear Tommy's voice ringing in my ears. Visions of the oxygenated blood gushed slowly out of Tommy's body and onto the brown carpet of the pastor's study.

This is what happens when you mess with my women.

The stranger's hands were large and strong as he wrestled with the two of us. The handgun concealed in his boot was braced with his second hand before it went off six times. We all fell to the ground simultaneously. Tommy, the musician, laid there, still holding onto the candid smile he had when he walked in.

The sound of the gun going off pierced my ears over and over again. The thought of losing someone I loved so intensely created shivers from my head to my toes.

Lord, I feel like I am about to pass out thinking about it. Disoriented, my stomach began to tremble.

It wasn't clear if prayer would change the situation or if running for cover would be the alternative plan. I gazed up at the stars and the moon as if they could talk to me. I felt unbalanced, heart racing, staggering, nearly falling, like I had been running for a lifetime. I hoped and prayed that no one from the church saw me like this but I couldn't seem to control my actions. I continued talking out loud to God for strength. My legs buckled before my knees hit the pavement.

"Lord, please, I need a miracle. Now." I looked up to the sky waiting to hear His voice as a fierce wind ran across my face. I once walked proudly with my head held high; now I wore the word shame across my forehead. "Where are you, God? Answer me!"

The urgent need to hear from God became a compulsive demand since 7:00 p.m. Right before the Sunday evening service it had all been a complete nightmare. I dreamed long ago that someone would hurt him eventually, but I didn't think it would be like this.

Stop! Don't shoot! I flashed back to the scene again. The truth of what really happened would remain hidden, hopefully. The church doesn't need the drama. I was pretty sure after touching that gun someone would blame me for all of this since Tommy came across as the charming and innocent one. I could not fathom the thought of going to jail and not being around my family. My stomach filled with butterflies thinking about it.

My dark blue, Ann Taylor designer suit, with silk lining, sagged away from my thin waistline and was dirty. My beige skin-toned stockings were ripped and practically nonexistent as lines went horizontally up my thighs, starting at my bare feet.

A few neighborhood-watch onlookers gathered on the sidewalk, whispering to each other, covering their mouths and shaking their heads. I guess they wanted to monitor me until the police came as one of them had his cell phone up to his ear speaking loudly.

What are they saying?

Trying to guess was nerve wracking as I wasn't good at reading lips. They must have thought I was another homeless person causing a ruckus in their neighborhood. But they didn't know, couldn't know.

Everyone focused on my outer appearance. They didn't seem to care about my state of mind. I was used to getting lingering stares due to my big eyes that people often said glowed along with my long mane of hair, and my beautiful skin. That was not how I was being assessed right now as my "good girl" image was tarnished, or shall I say nonexistent.

Raged from head to toe, I looked like a deranged criminal. "Jesus, help me!"

All they cared about was their ritzy neighborhood where swans strutted in front of their pretty lake and dogs had their own bathroom station. They looked as if they wanted to go back to being safe and sound again within their private community bubble. The way they crossed their arms and glared at me told the story that my personal troubles were not part of their community civic duty. They didn't seem convinced that they could help redeem or restore my sanity.

I didn't have the energy to tell them that I wasn't looking for trouble, I was just a preacher's daughter trying to make it into heaven despite my innocence being devoured by the enemy. I wouldn't harm a soul even if I wanted to. Normally I could preach my way out of sticky situations that might ruin my reputation. Give a bible verse or two or speak of God's goodness to take the light off of me during my moment of mess up. I had the gift of gab that always made people feel empowered, even when a situation was non-repairable. The "It" factor was what my father called it.

Not today, though; my thoughts were broken into a million pieces as I knelt feeling convicted and unprotected.

While I murmured prayers, a few individuals approached with caution, speaking softly.

"Ma'am, it's going to be okay whatever it is you're going through," one lady said.

"Yes, just calm down. We are here for you," the man with the cell phone responded. They stepped forward with the intention of modifying my out-of-control behavior. Several attempts to calm and soothe my delirium prompted my hand to go up in the air in defense and wave them off.

"Don't come near me, don't touch me, get away from me, Satan," I yelled.

"Ma'am, calm down, we just want to help you, what's wrong? What happened?" An older woman, wearing thick glasses and a colorful scarf around her neck stepped closer. "Aren't you Pastor Jones's daughter? Missy Jones, right?" She straightened her glasses and glared harder as she stepped into my personal space to assist. She seemed skeptical as she looked me up and down with curiosity.

Oh God, oh God. My identity had been exposed due to being the spitting image of my famous televangelist father. I jumped up off my knees and began to run in circles like a bat out of hell. I just couldn't stop envisioning a jail cell with padded walls and a roommate named Jezebel who licked her lips every other second. I bent down to put my face into my hands, terrified, knowing the old woman could see clearly enough through her bifocal glasses to identify me as a Jones girl.

"Ma'am, we've called the police to assist you, they'll be here soon. Whatever you did, they can help you," the old woman said as she scratched the hairs at the bottom of her chin, looking deeper into my soul.

"No one can help me now, ma'am," I replied as the tears cascaded down my cheeks. "I'm going straight to hell where I belong."

I gasped for air as my hands shook while reaching up to wipe away my tears. My feeble body leaned sideways, collapsing onto the cold ground. I landed with a thump as if I were a piece of play dough hitting the pavement hard. Everything continued to spin as blurry fragments of color sprinkled before me. The realization of being a possible suspect and being pinned to an imaginary cross flashed before me. Now I knew how Jesus felt.

I gasped for air again with an overpowering dry cough as my anxiety went into overdrive. If I told the truth to the police, I'd go down for the crime. But if I lied, the church would hate me. God would hate me.

Police sirens sounded in the distance as the blue and red lights inched closer and closer. A Durham City cop car with gold and white symbols drove up to the crowd and stopped abruptly as the officers charged toward me.

"Ma'am, I'm Officer Taylor. What's your name?"

"Does it matter?" I said, as I looked up at his square-shaped face with small lined lips.

The officer pulled out his black flashlight to examine my dilated pupils and asked, "Ma'am, do you want to tell us what happened? We're here to help you."

"You can't help me! Only Jesus can help me!" I screamed, before I jumped up trying to run but a female officer reached out to grab my arm. She swiped downward as her hand gripped my palm. I moved slowly while being escorted to the police car for a little privacy.

I leaned close to the car for balance when the female officer asked, "Ma'am, where are you coming from? It's obvious that you are not from around these parts. Do you remember what happened to you? Talk to us, we can help you."

I blurted out, squinting my eyes and still holding onto her firm grip, "I went to church today looking to preach the gospel, but before going into the service something horrible happened."

She looked at me sympathetically. "You can tell us. We're here to help. Can we call someone for you?"

The old woman leaned her head back with a gasp. "I knew it, she's a Jones girl! I remembered those big ol' eyes. I've seen her preach on television," she whispered to the neighbor standing beside her while tugging on her thick furry sweater to block the cold night air.

The officer held me close to her thick frame, leaning forward to catch the tears. Thankfully enough, she did not hear the old woman's comments and focused solely on me. Bloodstains remained smeared on my hands, legs and feet as the officer began to assess my entire body. She reached for a pair of gloves out of her pocket to begin an examination. She noticed that my left painted fingernails had a heavy build-up of scraped skin and fresh dirt. She moved my fingers around to evaluate the front and back of my hand. "Bloodied fingernails and hands are usually a telling story of a struggle, ma'am."

The only thing left to do was to bury my face in the officer's chest and pray that this would all go away. "It's complicated, officer." I was unable to control my sobbing as tears splashed from the top of my nose and cheeks onto her clean crisp blue uniform.

The other policeman patted my back as if he were burping a newborn baby. He looked down and asked, "What happened to your shoes?"

I ignored the question and continued praying silently, this time for vast speed that would allow me to zoom past him. Frantically, I plotted an escape in my mind as I kept my hand under my nose. After a few seconds of silence, I responded, "I... I don't know."

The female officer grabbed my right hand and peered closely at the other set of fingernails. "Is that blood also? I see you have discoloration in every fingernail. Ma'am, did someone try to hurt you?"

"Were you raped?" the other officer asked.

Still feeling dizzy and tired, I pulled my hand away. I was over all the questioning. I watched *The First 48* each week, so I was very familiar with the drill. I looked at them with widened, tired eyes, trying very hard to stay alert through the interrogation. I felt my lips quiver, but nothing came out of my mouth. A spasm shot up and down my spine, shaking my shoulders for several intense heartbeats. It was so dark, dreary and unclear. I put my head down and in a childlike tone, I whispered, "Help me please, Ms. Officer."

Come here baby, let me hold you. You know you love me. Don't worry about those other women. They are just lying on a brother. Tommy always told me that no one else mattered but me. Until today, I believed him. After years of speech classes, slowing down and concentrating were always the instructions given to me by my school speech pathologist. I tried to remember the technique while holding my head, but it didn't work. As I grew older anxiety became part of my being and using my hands became the alternative because I had no other way of exchanging information. I wished that I could motion how I felt or what I wanted to say at this moment. I was stuck. Talking with his hands worked for my daddy in the pulpit, but it was not something that I liked to do on a regular basis.

THAT CHURCH LIFE

I examined more flashing lights blinking before me, and then the darkness fell. Feeling light-headed, I hit the ground again.

Chapter 2

The officers tugged on my curled body. I felt the warm hand of the female officer on my shoulder as I looked up at her. "Get up, Miss!" They pulled me up as if they were lifting a big bag of weights. Suddenly, I saw pinches of light from the corner of my eye. My tongue ached from the hard fall, but my voice was able to whisper, "Call my pastor. Please, call my pastor. He'll pray for me and see me through this."

Blood rushed through my veins as a brand-new surge of energy formulated, giving me a small drop of strength. A few steps forward and a few steps back. Maybe a few steps away from the officers would stop the constant review of blood dripping down my legs. *Head hurts. I've got to get it together before they take me away.*

Tingling sensations tickled my arms as if the Spirit had hit me. *God, are you there? I know that's you, God. Answer me!* I needed God to help me break free from this situation.

I pushed, I shoved, and I broke loose from the officer's bondage. The onlookers stood with mouths open as they admired my great escape. They pointed and yelled, "She is fast!" I know all they saw were skinny, long legs dashing down the hill.

I was still in motion when I responded, "I'm not going to jail for anyone! God has given me favor for days like this!" I sprinted down the hill like a frightened animal.

The officers chased behind me. "Ma'am, stop! Please stop running, ma'am! We're here to help!"

Yes, I know it's you, Lord. Making a way out of no way once again! An intersection was up ahead. It was unfinished, so the asphalt turned to gravel and dirt which made a perfect exiting point.

God did that!

The misty clouds followed behind me as if they were imaginary angels that swooped over to protect me. Then, I heard, "Stop. Don't shoot her, man. Wait!" It sounded like the voice was just a few feet behind me. Another officer, trigger happy when dealing with a black person.

I knew this would all work out for my good in the end. The dirt and gravel dug into my bare soles, slowing my pace, but that was not going to stop me. I just needed to get to the end of the road. I planned to lose them once I entered Elmira Park.

I'm sure the police knew about the trail behind the middle school, but for some reason they didn't look for me there.

I have to be careful. I got this!

Like a magician, I vanished. All the years in track and field finally paid off. Behind a wild rose bush, near a steel fence, I hid. I remained tucked away from the officers as they tediously searched for me. That gave me time to think and a chance to catch my breath. *What should I do next?*

The officers' voices grew louder as a little voice spoke to me, "Sink into a fetal position and tuck your head."

I knew that was His voice!

The sun had now set completely as the darkness emerged, helping me to remain hidden. The beams of flashlights crisscrossed my hiding place, but they didn't see me. After a few minutes, they moved up ahead, still searching. It was time to pray and remain silent. I sat trembling in the bushes for hours.

It was now past midnight and I began to sit in a prostrated position for prayer, a ritual that I did daily. Daddy always said when you can think of nothing else, pray. The Lord's Prayer was fitting for that very moment.

"Our father which art in heaven…. Thy kingdom come, thy will be done…."

The weight of the day's events forced all remaining energy to leave my frail body. My sniffling morphed to sobbing again. Anger at Tommy's death made me pound the ground with my fists and my heels. I used my blue silk blouse as a tissue to wipe the tears away from my face.

Okay. Deep breaths. Happy thoughts.

THAT CHURCH LIFE

Church prayer meetings, pig pickings with the hog on a rotisserie stick over a grill and choir rehearsals all came to mind. Thoughts of Fifth Sunday Jubilee days and the love of watching all of the officials march down the aisle gave me a moment of peace.

Still, I kicked a few rocks around, mad at the world. "How did I get here, Lord? How did I get here?" I asked as I looked up to the sky for answers. I knew my family was worried sick. I was sure they were all over Durham looking for me.

Thoughts about my love for Christ and the church came to mind. I was compelled to recite Psalm 23:4.

"Yeah, though I walk through the valley of the shadow of death, I will fear no evil: for you are with me."

I didn't feel at all sensible yet. I felt like this was the end in what was supposed to be the beginning of my life. Tommy's big muscular arms always made me forget about my assignment from the Lord. He was like quicksand that sucked me in each time he came around me. He made me lose my way and lose my focus.

Over a man, really? Who does that?

I knew that my lust and love for him through the years slowly hindered my spiritual growth, but I just couldn't help myself. I no longer kept my eyes on God. Instead, I kept my eyes solely on him. *All my fault. I knew better. I was taught better. Can't blame the devil for this one.* If I'd listened and left that man alone, none of this would have happened.

"I'm going to miss you, Tommy. I'm sorry that this happened to you."

***

7:00 p.m., back in the study…

"Come here, girl, let me hold you," my boyfriend, Tommy, said.

He embraced me tightly. I was more than livid knowing he cheated again. He had been spotted by one of my church friends on several occasions going into the home of another church associate and staying all night. When I received the text message and pictures of his wrongdoings, I was devastated. I called him immediately. "Meet me before the evening service in the pastor's study. I know who you slept with last night."

He came immediately with an apologetic tongue knowing he couldn't lie about this one even if he tried. "Don't be mad at me, baby. We are in this forever," he said.

The door to the office opened slowly. A big, black dark shadow covered us as the stranger pointed his rifle.

Tommy turned his head as we immediately broke free from the embrace. "Aye, man, who are you? What are you doing back here?" "I'm a man that doesn't appreciate you sleeping with my women. That's who I am!" the stranger yelled.

THAT CHURCH LIFE

"Man, if you don't..." Before Tommy could complete his sentence, shots were fired. After we all fell to the ground, I felt the gun on the side of me. I picked it up and touched it, leaving my fingerprints all over it. I jumped up and ran out the door.

I peeled off parts of my church suit to use as a blanket. I laid in the grassy area of the trail to ease my back since I had nothing else I could use to rest my head on. The temperature steadily dropped during the sodium blue night and shivers migrated through my entire body. I placed my hands on my shoulders with the intent of staying warm. My head moved down close to the hard surface and the first thing I noticed was God's beautiful nature. The trees were bare and lifeless in the midst of fall season, but the branches hung downward looking strong and sturdy over my head. The dirt was dark and muddy as several beer cans remained scattered within a few feet of the massive bushes that covered me.

Maybe if I just close my eyes and go to sleep, I'll wake up and this will all be behind me. Surely, I'm dreaming, Lord.

Images of a bloodied curtain and walls continued to replay over and over again. Cured from asthma as a child, I learned to cope with conditions that would bother my breathing. But at that moment, I felt like that little girl on the track, taking two puffs of my inhaler before running for a victorious finish. My anxiety was on an entirely new level as my chest hurt and my breathing remained out of control.

Peace was in the woods of Elmira Park and no one would ever find me in such a secluded area. The only thing I heard was an owl, two trees across from my resting place and crickets jumping from one section of the grass to the next. I became agitated, feeling sticky as my stockings and suit were now pulled completely off while lying face down. My silk body shell hung off my left arm. I used my skirt to cover the other parts of my body, chanting in a whisper, "Forgive me, Lord, for I have sinned."

Deep down I wanted to stop saying the same thing, but I had lost all control of my tongue and thoughts.

What will my future look like after this murder? Could I survive the embarrassment? I didn't want this one bad experience to stay in my head. I had some really good times in church. I wanted to turn back the hands of time and listen to my pastor aka Daddy. He was right. I loved hard and always put God secondary when dealing with matters of the heart. I deserved to be punished for being such a fool. No more preaching the gospel, no more Fifth Sunday Jubilee, no more Sunday church dinners.

My comfort zone was singing. Music always seemed to help me through each day. I thought about the old Mothers of the church and their special requests for me to sing their favorite hymn every Missionary service. I giggled, twiddling with leaves as I sang the first song in the church hymn book. I knew every word, every phrase.

THAT CHURCH LIFE

Holy, Holy, Holy wasn't just a song sung in church on a regular basis. For me, it was also motivation during a horrible time.

"Holy, Holy, Holy...Lord, God almighty

Early in the Morning, our song shall rise to thee."

"I hear you, God, I hear you."

The spirit captured my emotions at that moment. God allowed me to rest safely in His arms as I rocked back and forth. Such a tragedy would bring division and doubt within the church walls. My gut told me God would protect and heal the hearts within the church after this crime. But the church and their "isms" otherwise known as rituals and learned habits weren't as important as his loss of life. I just witnessed someone dear to my heart expire in the pastor's study.

You know I love you girl, right? You are the only one for me. I could hear him say. I was exhausted. The only thing left for me to do was look up at the sky and say, "Rest easy, Tommy."

Chapter 3

The chilly night transformed into a warm dewy dawn that was much appreciated as I remained bare and feeling lifeless. I rolled over, amazed that I had slept on such a hard surface peacefully. I was glad to see another day.

Scents of tobacco floated and overpowered the redbud tree in front of me. I wondered why I didn't just end it all for myself instead of remaining on this hard ground.

Happy thoughts. Don't do this to yourself. It's not your time to leave this earth, girl.

My two-bedroom apartment near Duke University with great amenities was missed. Although home wouldn't feel serene and safe at a time like this. I was sure my cat, Twinkles, was lost without me. The only animal I knew that got anxious just like me.

There wasn't any movement in the trees; this area of town wouldn't come back to life until the boisterous school children stood on the door front of Sheppard Middle School directly in front of the trail.

THAT CHURCH LIFE

I can make it. Everything will be okay. I have to press on as I try to remain conscious. I can't say I have the joy of the Lord and think this way.

Mama always told me to think positive in times of trouble and God would do the rest. I missed hearing her soft soothing voice.

The sunshine landed on the pavement, beaming directly on my head. I stretched my arms wide as I stood and shifted my legs for proper circulation.

Moving slowly as if arthritis had grasped hold of my entire six-foot-three-inch body, I pulled on a tree branch for assistance. I missed my morning exercise routine and tried to pretend I was popping my workout tape into the DVD for a thirty-minute session. Images of Gilad, the mastermind of aerobics, appeared in front of me. He initiated my workout as I stretched every muscle to the max. I heard him say, "Get busy people. Don't let the muscle work you, you work the muscle!"

I snapped back to reality after less than three minutes of imaginary exercise. My stomach grumbled loudly, reminding me that it was time to end my unintentional fasting.

The city fish hut was right down the street and remnants of last night's fish fry mixed in with the fresh tobacco. The troubled acid in my stomach bubbled.

Looking down the opposite end of the street, I captured a glimpse of North Carolina Central University with the maroon and grey flag flying high in the air. It was chicken Monday for college students. I remembered enjoying my greasy chicken wings while on my way to class each week. I was starving!

Maybe if I returned home to change clothes, I could make it up to the school later for a good ole meal. Or maybe if I just brushed off my suit and put everything back on nice and neatly, no one would notice my odd appearance as I slipped by the crowd to grab a piece of chicken. Either way, I looked around and realized buying food wasn't an option, my purse was missing. Probably somewhere on the side of the road with my shoes.

I patted my head in frustration. I couldn't see my hair after laying flat on the ground all night, but I could feel the stringy strands of my spoofed natural all over my head. I felt homeless without having the bare essentials of my make-up compact, purse and accessories. I ran my fingers through the kinks as I patted my hair down flat. Life without a comb or brush was harsh. I became really concerned about dropping my blue Dooney and Bourke purse along the way.

I know material things don't matter, I'm trying, Lord. I am getting it together. But I did spend a lot of money on that purse, you know!

Michelle Hanks, a dear friend from my old high school church girl crew didn't live too far away from where I was hiding. Walking to her house was my only option with the hopes of catching her before going to work, since I didn't have my cell phone to call anyone. I needed a spare pair of shoes. Back in the day, I used to bring dress shoes to church to assist Michelle when she had only one pair of moccasins to wear no matter her outfit. I knew she would be there for me in spite of our fall out we had five years ago that continued to strain our friendship every now and again.

The calming light breeze settled my spirit while walking toward her home. "Hell, where is my purse?" I talked to myself the entire walk. "Lord, I just need you to help me. You said in your word that I am your child and with you, I am victorious. I don't know who that man was that pulled the trigger back at the church. But what I do know is someone is dead. I need you, Lord, for strength and courage. I need you for guidance. Father God, only you can see me through this."

My self-talk felt good and I kept it below a mumbling sound so that only God could hear my words.

I looked up realizing that I was almost to my destination as cars passed quickly on Avondale Drive. Morning traffic inched slower beside me as I looked straight ahead. *I feel nauseous.* I wobbled on the grassy area of the road as my knees knocked; I had to regain my balance. It was a challenge to focus on each step, but I had to so that my feet would not endure any more pain.

"I'm almost there, Lord. Thank you!"

I walked up to Michelle's home and looked up at her second-floor bedroom feeling nostalgic. *Can't wait to see her face.* We spent a lot of time in that bedroom over the years.

A major disagreement concerning the church had torn us apart. It was right after graduation and it was so petty, I couldn't remember all of the details. Since my memory failed me, I blamed it all on my head inflating after answering the call of ministry. I didn't remember if that was the real reason. I scratched my head, trying to recall all the details. I had reached out to Michelle a few years prior, longing for my girl crew again and we rekindled, attending various community activities together. But this was my first time visiting her home in over three years.

I remembered her room being the smallest in the house. The large body-sized posters of Fonzie from *Happy Days* and J.J. from *Good Times* hung on each side of her dresser drawers. Those 1980's television stars stood tall, taking up most of the wall space and fluttering every time the door opened. They stared at me each time I slept over. I wondered how much had changed since the last time I entered the Hanks's home. I also wondered about her family and if all eight of them still lived here.

I needed someone to comfort me. I wanted to be selfish for just an hour and think about my wants and needs only. Michelle would allow my tears to flow without judgment and give me the moments

I needed to clear my head. She would also allow me to release my emotions and then never mouth a word to anyone.

I walked up the front stairs on my tip toes, skimming my fingers up the hand rail. I tried to coax myself back to normal as I knocked on the wooden door with three gentle taps, hoping to get a quick response. As the door opened quickly, the welcoming of her wide smile made me happy.

"Oh Missy! Thank God you're okay. Everyone is so worried about you. Where have you been?" She grabbed me and held me tight to her chest. "Your dad called asking had I seen you. Lord knows he was sick about your disappearance and was looking all over Durham for you. You are all over the news this morning, you know that, right?"

"Give me a minute." I paused staring at her looking for a seat.

Minutes later she said in a whisper. "Talk to me Missy."

I paused, motioning my lips to move and then paused again.

She followed behind me. "Breathe sis. It's okay talk to me."

I became cognizant of my surroundings with a smidgen of energy. *Why didn't I come here last night? Why did I sleep on the ground?*

"I…I... I figured. I had to get out of there. You know I ain't used to hearing gunshots close range! I was right there next to the shooter.

The loud boom with gun powder sprinkling everywhere tore my nerves up, girl. Being terrified is an understatement."

Michelle sat and listened as she braced her hand across her chest. "I can't even imagine. What happened?"

"A man came in while Tommy and I were in the study right before service. Tommy got caught with his women and the man came in shooting. We fell so hard to the ground all at one time. I rolled to check Tommy's pulse and blood gushed out all over me. The gun was beside me and I put my hand all over it not thinking that my fingerprints were now the last prints to touch the gun."

"What?" Michelle shrieked.

"Yes, girl! The shooter was nice enough to leave me alive as I ran out the door. A part of me wishes he would have taken me out, too, so that way I wouldn't have to deal with all of this. I couldn't see his face, he had some type of weird mask on, but I wasn't sticking around to take the blame. I knew that I would be framed as the jealous or deranged girlfriend if I stayed there with my fingerprints everywhere and all that blood and gunpowder on my shoes."

"Framed? Girl, now you know that would not be the case. You need to stop watching *Scandal* late at night. Why would someone want to frame you? I'm sure the police would have figured out who's fingerprints touched the gun first. Everyone knows how much you love that lame. Running away was not going to stop the questions nor take the pain away, honey." Michelle began to assess my entire body as her voice hit a high pitch. "We need to call your dad so he can be at ease. Look at you, your clothes are ripped, your feet are stained and blood is everywhere. I'm surprised someone didn't stop you while walking down Alston Avenue. Let me fix you some food while you call your father. You hungry?" Fixing food to ease the pain was a southern hospitality thing. She was so concerned with feeding me, yet she wasn't worried about Tommy. She stared at the massive amount of blood on my legs while shaking her head. I dropped my eyes midway and began to stare at the living room walls in an attempt at gathering my thoughts. I lost focus on what she was saying as I continued to scan several pictures of the holy cross in different sections of the room. The pictures were different shapes and sizes as if they were purposefully collected to show the variations of the holy cross. I didn't understand why anyone needed a picture of it surrounding every living room wall. I assumed they needed extra reminders of Jesus's sacrifice for our sins. I glanced back at Michelle.

The house had been upgraded since my last visit. There was a display of black figurative little people on a shelf and black art pieces which were high quality. A sun deck had been built and added that connected to the living room. It had an indoor screen so that the beautiful, large plants obtained maximum lighting as they surrounded the leather furniture and seventy-inch plasma television. This was a major status change compared to the days of the hand-me-down recliners with torn fabric and cotton balls coming out of the seams. Their twenty-first century farming had made a difference in their lives. Michelle's family had become wealthy from selling their home-grown vegetables and chickens. I regained my focus. The room spun rapidly as all the fixtures began to look as one. I felt dehydrated. "Do you have something to drink?" I asked as my voice trembled.

Michelle walked into the kitchen, opened the pantry and pulled out a bottle of water. She came back into the living room and sat down. "Here you go, sis." She slid the bottle across the coffee table as I leaned forward slowly to grab it.

I responded to her question about food while taking a sip of water, feeling sluggish. "No, by the way, I haven't had anything to eat. I've been hiding in Elmira Park all night. I didn't want the police to come back looking for me and I didn't want to go home alone like this. My mind was all messed up. I just needed to get my thoughts together and shake off some of this anxiety. I lost my purse, so I don't have any medication. So, is he...?" I asked as I tapped my leg in nervousness. Michelle looked up and knew exactly what I was asking.

"What? Is he dead?"

"Yes, is Tommy...dead?" I stuttered.

With a look of disappointment, Michelle paused and took a deep breath. "Unfortunately, I don't have any answers for you, sweetie. After that last beatdown you took from him, Tommy should have been six feet under long before the shooting. But knowing that fool, he has nine lives and probably sitting up somewhere sipping on a tea lemonade mix." She sat down, putting her elbow on the table and her hand on her neck.

I placed my hands over my mouth in shock that Tommy, the love of my life, could possibly be alive to see another day. The comments she'd made about my last beatdown were not acknowledged right away. I didn't expect Michelle to be so abrasive. What was that about? "I started the fights, can't blame him for hitting me back," I responded in defense. Then, quickly, I added, "Well, let's drive down to the church to see if he is alive. What are we waiting for?"

"I think you should call Pastor Jones and let him know you're okay first. I'm sure he's still worried sick about you."

A frown came over my face. Deep down I didn't care how my daddy felt concerning this situation. I only wanted to know if Tommy lived or died. "Daddy will be all right. If he didn't try to come to my rescue all the time, this would have never happened."

"Well, thank God he always does or else you would be a dead woman!" Michelle gave a blank stare as she seemed to wonder why I still had feelings for Tommy and why I still gave a hoot about a man who had made it a habit to put his hands on me. She looked disappointed in the choices I made for myself. It was written all over her face and she rolled her eyes every time I spoke his name. Definitely not the responses I envisioned before arriving on her doorstep.

Trying to change the subject, she grabbed my hand and swung me away from the living room sofa. "Well, let me get started on fixing you something to eat," she said as she guided me to the linen closet. "While I'm cooking, you need a shower. Hopefully after you get some food in your boney body, you'll be ready to go see your family."

She opened the linen closet next to the kitchen door and grabbed two towels. I continued to admire the changes to the house by examining the wall-to-wall carpet, plush leather furniture, hard wood floors in the front foyer and the new deck scenery. Plush upgrades.

I grabbed the towels and hugged her tight, silently grateful for her love and hospitality. I was so happy to see her pretty dark brown face as oil glistened from her forehead. I laid my head down on her shoulder as I stretched downward to reach the tiny arms attached to her five-foot-five-inch frame.

I pondered, still wondering if Tommy were among the living. Although he did bad things from time to time, he was still a good guy. I spent a lot of time trying to "fix" him. All he needed was a little more guidance and prayer.

Looking down with sorrowful eyes, I felt loved. "I love you, sis."

"I love you, too, sweetie. I want you to get some counseling when all of this is over, okay? Just because we know Jesus doesn't mean we're immune to the cares of this world. That man has taken over your brain and you are *different*. I can't continue to watch him make a fool out of you. Do you hear me, woman of God?"

I rubbed her upper arm and said, "I know, I know."

Trying hard not to make any eye contact, I limped to the bathroom with my matching towels and prepared myself for a nice clean, hot shower. I reached for the water valve and turned it gently to the left. I enjoyed the cold droplets that spurted out before the hot water could transfer. I considered it to be my liquid sunshine as it dripped on my face. I was happy to finally bathe and couldn't wait to check on Tommy.

I rushed quickly to shower as the lukewarm water dripped down my back. I could smell the food from downstairs. It reminded me of when my mother used to cook me breakfast every morning before school. But I knew I wasn't going to have time to eat it. I had to find out sooner than later about my man.

Once I felt zestfully clean, I walked into Michelle's room energized, with a towel wrapped around me.

Michelle walked upstairs and entered her room and took me into her closet as I rushed to find the right outfit.

She examined my hairstyle, reaching up trying to fix it, and wasn't a bit concerned that I was anxiously trying to get back to the church. "It's going to be all right, Missy. I know it's tough for you to grin and bear it all but seriously, if we find him alive, you really need to leave that man alone. Church folks are always talking and they don't understand how such a pretty woman in ministry continues to deal with such a loser." She rubbed the back of her neck.

"I don't care what others think about him. The church has controlled my life for too long. They're the reason why my mother died of cancer feeling alone and mistreated. After all she did for them rascals and they still killed her off softly. I am so sick of hearing the judgmental remarks of folks that are probably going to hell in a hand basket anyway." I put my head down, pulling away as she attempted to put a brush to my hair. I was hoping that we would change the subject. Thinking about it slowed me down a bit. I was tired of the same old speech. "No one really understands what I go through just to get through each Sunday without becoming violent, especially after I think about what they did to my mom."

"Well, how are you going to be an example of Jesus to others when your life is so out of the will of God?" She crossed her arms. "People in Durham look up to the Jones family and they travel from near and far to hear you preach. How could you take on that kind of attitude considering that you have a responsibility to represent God? Truth be told, that's why I started attending St. James Baptist. The

Baptists don't have these kinds of troubles." I put on the dress picked out for me and rolled my eyes.

"Wait. Wasn't Jeffrey Dahmer a Baptist?"

"There is always an exception to the rule. But for a place where God is the main focus, why is there always drama?"

"There's drama in every church. No one on this earth has a perfect church, believe that. At the beginning of the day, we are still human and subject to make mistakes. We are all humans that fight our flesh daily." I tried to remain calm as I noticed a Mona Lisa painting above the closet. "Mona Lisa? Why do you have her in your room?" I chuckled, not understanding the relevance of the painting in a room that still had representation of Fonzie and J.J.

With bulging eyes, she swung her head around. She seemed proud of her art collection. "You need to get with the program and become well rounded. I like all types of art. That is one picture that is needed in every home."

I wrinkled my nose, looked at the picture, then back to Michelle. We both threw our heads back in laughter. Even she knew that having those three pictures together was a silly concept. "She doesn't go with any other art work in this room. I don't think J.J. needs the competition." I laughed.

"As ugly as J.J. is, he better be lucky that someone else wants to be in the same room with him at all."

After getting dressed, I finally made the call to my dad.

When he answered, I said, "Hello, Dad?"

His voice trembled as he coughed between his words. "Missy, is that you?"

With a sigh of relief, I said, "Yes, Daddy, it's me."

I was considered Daddy's protégé and he cherished our relationship. He wanted me to become a famous pastor like him one day by building an even bigger platform for our televangelist ministry. I could get lost in a worldly mess behind closed doors, but I dared not show it to the public. As long as I remained the golden child on TV, he didn't bother me much.

"Missy, what happened? When you didn't come out of the study to preach, I came looking for you. I found that boy lying in the middle of the floor."

I thought about what the crime scene must look like. "Daddy, I didn't know what to do. I made a mistake and wrapped my hands around that gun after that strange man came in and shot Tommy. I just knew I would be in deep trouble with my fingerprints everywhere. I felt like I was doomed for jail if I sat around that office in all that blood."

"Honey, but if you didn't do anything, why would you worry? Why would you go to jail? That's nonsense. You know I would have been there for you no matter what."

I began tapping my leg as my anxiety kicked in again. "Daddy, I am so scared, I don't know what else to do. Is he…?"

I heard a pause through the phone. "I guess you want to know if that yeller Negro is still living, huh?" he asked as his voice escalated to another level.

"Yes."

"Shame on you. That's the least of your worries. That fool is at Duke Hospital getting all the tender loving care he needs from the nurses. I'm sure he is soaking up every minute and hasn't thought about you, not one second, my dear." Dad began to use his sarcastic voice that always seemed to show up when you least expected it.

Michelle whispered in the background, "I told you he was worried." With my arms folded, I continued to listen to my daddy babble. He was glad that Tommy's ex-girlfriend's jealous baby's daddy got to him before any of our family members did. Tommy Lee Davis was a light skinned brother, with light brown eyes and Indian curly, fine hair that he wore shaped into a round afro. He was tall, sleek and sported a thick, untamed beard that seemed to make him more ravishing and debonair to the church ladies. He was bowlegged and loved to lean his legs out so that the indent within his knees would show. When he grinned, his teeth glistened like the moon. One would assume that he never missed a dental appointment. He smelled like Polo cologne and soap for men no matter the day of the week. The ladies loved Tommy and Tommy loved the ladies.

He had a reputation that did not warrant commitment. His sly behavior caused trouble throughout the years, from women fighting over him, to family members threatening him and even destroying his personal items. This go round of his careless sex games caught up with him. He'd made love to a woman who had a jealous baby's daddy.

I grabbed the kitchen chair, pushing it in front of me while trying to maintain my balance. "At his point, I guess you're right. It's all said and done with now and he has shown me what he is about. I'm just glad he isn't dead, that's all."

I could tell my dad's hands were in motion as he was known to move them around while talking. "Don't try to be a rock for me, honey, I know you. Why would you want a fool like that to still be in your life? You trying to play tough right now, but I know you will break your neck to go and see him. I'm sure you were in the pastor's study all kissy, kissy with him and this man comes in and tries to kill him dead. That man could have shot you, too! Thank God the shooter got the hell out of dodge. Instead of being in there with that nut, you should have been praying before you brought the word. But no, uh-uh, not you, you want to be Mrs. Davis so bad, huh?"

I was disappointed that I was being scolded before I could even look at my daddy eye to eye after such a horrid situation. "I'm so hurt that you feel this way, Daddy. I give the church all of me so no one should have anything to really say about it. I can't help who I love."

With an instant response, he came back with, "Oh yes the hell you can! Forgive me, Lord! Girl, you have lost your cotton pickin' mind. You better not go up there to that hospital to see about that triflin' nigga either." Sometimes his preacher talk would shift from proper dialect to Ebonics in less than ten seconds when provoked. "You hear me, gal? He's probably in the hospital bathroom closet with a woman sitting on his lap as we speak. Don't say I didn't warn you. Lord have mercy! Please give my baby strength, Jesus."

I whimpered, "I know, I know." He was not ashamed to tell it like he saw it. He knew I would do anything to justify my relationship. "I gotta go, Dad. I'm going up to the church to help out. I'm sure it's a mess," I said as I stuffed more grits and eggs into my mouth no longer worried now that I heard Tommy was amongst the living.

"Listen, if you get to the church and the investigators ask questions, don't hesitate to answer. I will see you later, baby girl," he said in a lower tone.

I began to cry again. As I wiped the tears off my cheeks, I responded, "Love you, Daddy."

"Love you, too, baby girl."

Michelle stood over me pouring more grits onto my plate. She looked down with the pot in her hand, ready to pour more if needed.

I stood up to put the phone back on the hook that was attached to the kitchen wall. I was walking back to my seat as my eyes zeroed in on my plate.

She rubbed my back as I sat down and said, "It's really going to be okay, my friend. Let's go to the church and see if they need anything and then we will pay Natalia a visit."

I crammed the rest of my food into my mouth and moved away from the table slowly as I contemplated eating more. Feeling discombobulated, I could only imagine what the rest of the day would be like.

Natalia was also part of my church girl crew and she always had my back. She worked for Delta Airlines and started traveling right after high school in pursuit of seeing the world. Whenever she was in town, we always met up for girl talk and laughter. Dying to know what was being said about me in the streets, while walking toward the door, I asked, "Does Natalia know about any of this?"

Batting her eyes and rubbing her side nervously, Michelle said with slight hesitation, "Girl, now you know if Natalia knew about your short sabbatical, she would have put an APB out on you."

"Yeah, I could see that happening. She doesn't play those hide-and-go-seek games. She would have found me hours ago."

Michelle leaned over, pressing against my arm as I looked down. "Let's go, girlfriend, before she finds out through someone else. I'm sure Mother Smithfield has gotten ahold of half of Durham with her gossiping self. You don't want to hear Natalia's mouth, trust me."

I nodded in confirmation, saddened at the thought of giving Natalia the details. "You're right about that! I don't need any more drama in my life right now."

Chapter 4

Five years earlier…

It was at North Carolina Central University where we first met. I was sitting on the sorority wall with a couple of friends and called Natalia and Michelle to stop by to eat dinner with me in the school cafeteria. They came to visit often as they enjoyed the food prepared at the school. It wasn't your ordinary cafeteria as they had over one hundred items on their salad bar and it was opened to the public for all meals.

I took them to my favorite spot in the cafeteria, so we could chat, laugh, and cut up without being disturbed. And there he was… Tommy Lee Davis. He passed by our table with a group of football players wearing his pants loosely fitted and his Tommy Hilfiger underwear band showing.

I looked over, eyeballing his slender physique and no longer paying attention to the girl chatter. He had thick arms and a slender waist that was in proportion with his thin legs.

"Hey, Tommy baby!" Michelle yelled.

"What's up, homey?" He waved with a grin, moving a few feet backwards to view the entire table.

You know him?" Natalia spoke loudly.

"Yeah, he's a musician. I know most of the musicians around here. He is one of the most popular ones because he can really play."

"Who are your friends?" he asked Michelle, patting her shoulder.

"This is Missy and Natalia."

He glanced over Natalia and shifted his gaze directly to my eyes.

"Well, hello, beautiful." I blushed as he came closer to my side of the table.

"Pastor Jones's daughter, right?" he asked.

"Yep."

"Uh-huh. You look just like him. I watch your church on television all the time. Nice to meet you." He took the deepest swallow I had ever seen as his Adam's apple jumped up and down.

I grinned, breathing heavily and inching farther down into my seat becoming very bashful due to his presence.

"You are so beautiful," he said with a slow and sexy tone. He reached over to shake my hand. My teeth clinched with nervousness. Our hands connected and locked together tightly. I wanted to melt as he put my hand up to his mouth. He kissed it tenderly and said, "This must be my lucky day."

I felt an electric spark shoot from my fingertips all the way down my abdomen. "Nice to meet you as well, Tommy. Thank you for the compliment." I snatched my hand back, trying to play it cool as I became even more nervous by the second.

Michelle looked at me with a blank stare. I scanned his entire body and looked back at her. His body structure was breathtaking.

What a man, what a man!

He was flawless in my eyes. He burned holes through my bosom zooming in on my breasts. I shivered.

He continued to pierce his fiery eyes deeply into my inner core. I exhaled, remaining composed as butterflies rumbled in the pit of my belly.

"Yo, Tommy?"

A random guy wearing stone-washed jeans, blue Air Force One shoes, and a blue Nike hat yelled across the room. He lifted his hands up in the air asking in a familiar sign language of "What's up, what's taking you so long to get over here?"

Tommy turned around sharply as his blue Sperry shoes swerved sideways. He wore the finest designer clothes with creased, ironed jeans.

Tommy didn't respond as he continued beaming down my shirt while he pulled his pants up on his waist.

Out of nowhere, Tommy blurted, "I've got to have you all to myself."

You are the finest female on campus. I bet you got a man, don't you?"

I shrugged now feeling uncomfortable.

"I've got to have you, shorty," he said in a deep voice.

I smirked and put my head down. With my voice shaking, I asked, "So you're in a fraternity I see." I stared at the jacket he held in his hand that matched the colors of his outfit. "Are you a freshman? I've never seen you before."

The question caught him off guard as he doubled back with bulging eyes. He reached in his pockets, looking nervous.

"This is my first semester here. I transferred from Durham Tech. This is my third year in school."

"Oh nice." I moved my head up and down acknowledging that I was still listening as we continued to stuff fresh salad with over ten toppings into our mouths.

"I'm coming to visit your church one day. I've been there a few times with the Fifth Sunday Jubilee, but I don't recall laying my eyes on you and all this beauty," he moaned, as if I was a sweet piece of cinnamon bun that had just tickled his palate. My eyebrows crinkled as sweat beads filled my brow from his presence.

"Do you sing?" he asked, his dimple curving deeper into his cheek.

"Of course, I can sing. What preacher's kid do you know that doesn't sing or play an instrument?" He shrugged as we laughed.

"One day you'll be singing for me." He looked around as his boys were in the background clowning him for leaving them to talk to a girl.

"What does that mean?" I asked.

He pulled a business card out of his wallet and handed it to me. It read, *Tommy Lee Davis, Musician Extraordinaire.* I giggled, not knowing what to say.

"Girl, if you don't stop with all that giggling," Natalia whispered.

"Thank you for your card. Nice meeting you, Mr. Tommy."

"It was a real pleasure meeting you as well, Ms. Jones. I'll be seeing you again real soon, lil' mama." He stood straight, folding his jacket in his arms as he made a face at Natalia.

Michelle leaned back in her seat and said as she wiped the ranch dressing from her salad off of her cheeks, "Don't tell me you are considering calling him."

"We'll see," I responded. "He is cute!"

"I hope you use your good sense and throw his card away. All you're doing is asking for trouble," Natalia said.

"How do you know?" I asked.

"Let's just say a lot of people know him. He gets around," Michelle responded without looking up.

Who cares! He is fine!

THAT CHURCH LIFE

Chapter 5

We drove up to Mt. Zion Holy Church where Pastor Henry Jones, aka Daddy remained the Shepherd for the last fifteen years. As the black Lexus truck pulled up slowly beside the large crowd, we saw members holding hands in unity at the front gate.

Based upon their bizarre looks of disgust, I gathered that members were angry due the extent of damage caused by the crime investigation. They probably wondered who was responsible for violating the sacred boundaries of the church. I'm sure they didn't like the fact that the holy grounds of Mt. Zion had been doused and tarnished with sinful acts.

Blood was everywhere. I never came out to preach that night. I am sure they heard the gunshots while in the congregation. A million and one reasons why they would be highly upset.

They were not able to pray inside the building as desired, due to all the yellow tape and blood stains that remained on the back walkway. They stood patiently, waiting for clearance before crossing over into the church yard.

The Durham City Police, private investigators and forensics specialists crawled around the building cleaning up remains of bullet shells and anything else they could find that would help the case.

Mother Smithfield, one of the oldest and well-respected church members, stood in front of the gate talking to other church members when she turned completely around after hearing the sound of a vehicle behind her. She had a livid expression that identified sheer frustration. She looked back at the sanctuary and shouted, "In all my thirty years of attending this church, I ain't never seen no mess like this. We need to pray that our musician is still amongst the living and that the violence will cease in our city!"

The church members agreed and responded, "Amen!"

"Let us pray right where we stand." She bowed her head for prayer as the other members shuffled around her. "Let's form a circle to show this community what unity looks like." They grabbed hands as she took the lead. She prayed with one eye opened and one eye closed, trying to watch everything around her.

"Father God, we come to you right now praying for the victims of this horrific crime, Lord Jesus. We ask that you release your angels of protection around them, Lord God. We don't want them demon-filled criminals to come back to bother us ever again, Lord God. Continue to keep this church covered. Keep us safe under your blood, Jesus. In Jesus' name we pray. Let the church say, Amen."

"Amen!"

THAT CHURCH LIFE

She dropped her prayer partner's hands in disgust while eyeballing me as we stepped out of the GS 460. "She is probably one of the reasons why that sweet young man got shot. May God's hand strike some sense into both of their warped, sex-filled, backsliding minds."

I stepped closer, overhearing the nasty little comment she'd made. We continued to walk forward, ignoring the whispers. My head was lifted completely up as I walked with confidence and grace. The investigators didn't seem to realize that I had any involvement with the case based on their non-responsiveness to my appearance. No one came to me with questions nor did they look up at the crowd as they used little brushes to sweep across the back door. They completed their task shortly after and signaled to the deacons to open up the front gate.

The steel iron gate flew open as the crowd marched in. They carried on as if they were in Selma, Alabama walking for freedom. Hands lifted to the sky, heavy stomps hit the pavement. I walked along with the crowd stopping beside the remaining yellow tape that hung across the front door steps. I was ready to address the people with positive words, just like Daddy taught me. "Greetings family and friends! It is with great sorrow that we are gathered here today. I expected my father to be here to address the issue. But since there is no sign of him here yet, I will speak in his stead. I must say, this is the first time something so tragic has come right to our front door.

The commotion staggers the word that God had for His people. I tell you, I was so prepared to preach yesterday and Lord knows I did not expect such a tragic outcome. I planned to preach about saints continuing to build faith despite the storms in their lives. I now know that it was truly a Godsend and timely word that we needed to hear. Through all of this, we stand here together, building our faith right now here today. Tragedies such as this teach us to hold onto God's unchanging hand."

Mother Gaines lifted her cane up high in the air and shouted, "Hallelujah. Say it, say it, gal. Yeah God!"

I continued. "Only God can fight this battle and with Him we can do all things that He may strengthen us. Don't be discouraged nor be dismayed. After all we've been through, we can only get better as each challenge brings new blessings. He protected us from harm and danger. There may have been a crime committed in the back, but He protected all of you while you were in the front. Can I get a witness?"

The crowd responded as if we were inside the church doors having a real service. "He watched over us despite what it all looks like around us! Hallelujah!"

Mother Gaines tapped her cane in the grassy area as she wobbled back and forth. "Hallelujah, gal, hallelujah!"

I felt the Holy Spirit take full control as I continued raising my hands in the air. Michelle stood behind me within my shadow. She was proud and stood tall watching God move through my words.

I continued with a scripture. "We are made to endure for a night but joy cometh in the morning! All things are truly working for our good. This too shall pass!"

The church folk clapped their hands feeling strong again from my passionate words and shouted in unison, "Glory, Hallelujah!"

Right smack dab in the middle of my comeback speech, I began to clutch my heart feeling happy for such a welcomed response. I saw specks of light blink in front of me. I started to hear voices. It was Tommy's voice and it was clear. It was as if he was standing right in front of me.

I love you Missy. Echoed.

I shuffled my feet looking around hoping to see his face. Within seconds, the trees and clouds started spinning as they reached out to one another. I heard faint voices in the distance screaming, "Somebody call an ambulance and help her!"

Chapter 6

Waking up in a thin, sheeted, flat hospital bed is not something to be proud of. I thought I was an asset to the church, giving them positive words by clearing their hearts and minds and easing the pain of the situation. But suddenly within an instant, I became a medical liability. I scanned the room, examining the big white board hanging in front of me with the room number and nurse's name written in blue cursive. The tiny bathroom stall stood directly across from the foot of the bed. The door remained open as I assessed a urine cup hanging off the rim of the toilet and a big trash can on the side wall.

Visions of how romantic Tommy used to be formulated. He was such a gentleman when we first met. There was nothing I would not do for that man. The first few times I confronted him about other women he would brush it off convincing me that there was no way possible he would ever do me wrong.

"Don't believe what you hear, Missy. Those girls are just jealous. Always hating on my girl," he would always say.

My interest shifted as I looked down at my forearm and stared at the long IV with white tape holding it in a stiff position at the center of my wrist. The corners of my eye captured a big fluffy recliner that sat right beside my bed. In it, sat my daddy who looked over at me; I guess he heard me shifting in the bed and looked up.

He leaned forward as his curly black hair shimmered under the room's lighting, and his rugged beard, dingy and untamed, brushed his shoulder. He reached for my hand as he shook his head back and forth in a brief silence.

"Gal, one day you gonna learn that you can't be everything for everybody. I should have told you not to take your hind parts up there to the church. You could have waited a day or two or at least until you felt better."

My eyes drifted while trying to refocus and not puke up all of the liquids they were putting inside of me.

"What happened?" I asked. "How did I get here?"

"That anxiety got the best of you, gal," Daddy responded.

That figures.

Always laying in a hospital bed due to this awful illness they call anxiety. "Daddy, you know I can't go one day without trying to make things right for our people. I felt bad they had to go through all of that because of me. It's an emotional roller-coaster. Do they know?"

Daddy answered abruptly, "No, they don't know all the details, gal. You paranoid! No one knew that you were in the study at the time of the shooting but me. All they knew was you had to preach that night. So, you better take it to your grave." He gave me a stern look.

"You know I wouldn't let the congregation be privy to that information, Daddy."

"Better not! They will never look at you the same again. All we got in this world is our name and I will protect that until I take my last breath."

"The more I think about it, Daddy, I realize that I should not be walking around here ashamed of something that didn't really pertain to me. This didn't happen because of anything I did wrong so why does it matter if they know or not?"

"Gal, all of this happened because of your man being irresponsible and not caring about his actions. Boyish games played with all these women are dangerous." He patted my hand and laid it down on by my side gently.

I rolled over on my left hip, feeling overwhelmed and depressed as I brushed my cold feet onto the foot board and moved a few of my pillows underneath the covers looking for heat. "Life's too short, Daddy. I'm going to get this thing right one day."

Daddy released a strange glare filled with sarcasm as his forehead wrinkled. "You don't say?"

"Stop trying to make me laugh," I said as I giggled like a teenage girl at his expression.

"You know I try very hard to keep a good Christian image while they still talk about me like a dog at church. But I know I got to push through it." My laughter turned to tears thinking about all the sacrifices made by the Jones family for the congregation.

He rubbed his chest. "You the most crying woman I've ever seen. How you go from laughing to crying? Stop all that, gal."

"No matter what I do, they will still view me as the rebellious, out of control, spoiled preacher's kid. Nothing more, nothing less."

"Trust me, I understand what you're going through, baby girl. Me and your mama went through the rain, sleet, snow and storm during our early years in ministry, too. We already know folks don't care about their brother or sister like they should anymore. It has become a narcissistic world in the church house. But you are doing what you do, not to please them, but to please God!" He rubbed his hand across his beard as he crossed his legs getting comfortable. "Now, you got to realize that you haven't had a good track record with men, am I right?"

I blinked and sighed because I knew what was coming next. "Yes, Daddy, dating has always been a challenge."

He continued with his speech, "You must understand that it doesn't look good when you are blessed beyond measure and continue to bring knuckleheads to the church."

"I know, I know."

He held his hand on his chin as he went down the list. "I tell you what, you have dated Durham's finest milk duds over the years." We both laughed reaching back into our memory banks.

"First, it was peanut head Brian Kemp who was a Jehovah's Witness and you should've known that wasn't going to last long." He shook his head.

"He was really nice, Daddy."

"Well, niceness from someone that ain't of the same faith doesn't work when you're a minister in a holiness church."

"I figured that out, Daddy."

"Then it was Thaddeus Jenkins from the projects. I could no longer take his Jeri curl-flying, gangster-limp walking, pig-feet eating, toxic bad breath-breathing boy around me any longer. So glad you got rid of him, too. You better not tell nobody about that one either, gal! Some things you should keep between you and Jesus." His eyebrows caved in looking serious as he summoned me to secrecy.

I took a deep breath as he continued.

"And what about that other one…what was his name?"

I sat up straight to respond. "Who, Rico?"

Daddy sat back, snapping his fingers in confirmation. "Yes, that doggone Rico Shaw. The ugliest little black boy I had ever laid eyes on in all my days! His teeth were all over the place and he had the nerve to put a gold cap on the top front tooth. Every time he came to the house, I couldn't look him in the eye without looking at his jacked-up grill."

"Daddy, please—"

"He always came to church with his Boston Red Sox hat on his head, being just plum disrespectful. Bet he ain't never seen not one part of Boston either! No home training at all. But yet my baby girl, the youth minister and choir director, that everyone loves to watch, was infatuated with that nappy-headed nigga named Rico."

I closed my eyes and remained silent. I knew once Daddy got started with the humiliation speeches, he couldn't stop. He laughed at his own jokes as he recanted my life. Thankfully, the door swung open and I looked up to see who was on the other side of the wooden frame.

Michelle and Natalia walked in with a Cobb salad, a slice of cheese pizza and a twelve-ounce cherry coke. They knew what I liked as I followed the food from the door to the table. I was tired of listening to Daddy and ready to eat.

"Hey, sweet thang!" Natalia shouted as she popped her bubblegum in her mouth, placing a stack of napkins near the food.

"Wow, look at all this food. The Lord answered my prayers. Thanks for thinking of me, girls."

Michelle pulled out a fork and spoon and placed it in front of me. "You know how we do it. Food and friendship go hand in hand. Have some, pastor?"

"Nah. Just feed baby girl. She needs every bite of it." He chuckled.

Natalia's eyes traveled to the cuts and bruises on my ear. "What happened to you, honey? You look like someone that's been in a cat fight. I thought you were only here because you had an anxiety attack. What's with all the bruises?"

My dad and Michelle exchanged looks and then looked back at me to see if I would confess my troubles. I knew that Natalia would flip once she got a whiff of the story. I tried to formulate my words and started my sentence slowly, "Let's just say it was a very long night." I put my head down, staring at the salad while trying to avoid eye contact.

"A long night with who?" she questioned as she stood over me, looking around for answers.

"Something happened yesterday that was out of my control, right before evening service. I'm sure you were on a plane flying somewhere at the time. It was nothing." I took a sip of my cherry coke and gazed over at Michelle in hopes of getting some kind of help with this one.

Natalia squared her shoulders and lifted her head. "Well. somebody better tell me what's up in this piece before it gets ugly. You sitting up here with an IV hanging, bruises everywhere and hair sticking straight up like a peacock and you think I'm not going to keep asking questions? You have lost your ever-loving mind. I need to know what the hell is going on, now!" Her hands flew up as if she was using her flight attendant techniques to get her point across. "I'm tired of church folks and all their secret gardens and closets. Spill it or I will start making some phone calls. You don't want me to call Mother Smithfield. I know she got the juice."

Daddy burst into laughter holding his stomach, and said, "Sophia's home, yes Sophia's home," as he imitated a line from the movie *Color Purple*.

Natalia was the boss of all of us. She didn't mind going off on a regular basis as her head rolled and her arms remained folded. "Glad to have you home, gal! Natalia Freeman, the loudest daughter that I claim. Good to see ya!"

Michelle said, "Lord have mercy you must have high blood pressure with all that fire spitting out of your big mouth."

"Now you know that gal ain't gonna tell you what happened, so let me have the honors," Daddy said, bracing his leg as if he was about to preach. Natalia wrinkled her nose as she sat down to hear the story with watery red eyes. She didn't like being left out and you could tell it hurt her feelings to find out such important information at the last minute. She blew out air from her mouth, breathing heavy as she attempted to count to ten. She was taught in anger management classes that breathing slowly was a good way of taking control of her emotions.

"I'm waiting, Passa," she said as her arms remained folded.

Daddy started moving his hands around. "Well, your sister over here can't seem to leave our curly head musician alone. I knew I should have fired him years ago when I caught him winking at her during one of the Fifth Sunday Jubilees. Makes no sense that someone on the organ, playing for every service, ain't a bit more saved than the man on the moon."

"Amen to that," Michelle said.

I swung my neck around as my eyes bulged during Daddy's commentary. "Listen to you. You hired him," I said in disgust.

Daddy continued to flare up his hands as he finished the story. "But that is beside the point. Anyway, his hoe tendencies have finally caught up with his bowlegged tail."

I could see the steam coming out of Natalia's ears as her eyes widened while tilting her head. "Um, what are you talking about, Passa? What happened? I need more details than what you're giving right now."

Daddy continued, "You remember that girl Lola that used to go to St Mark's years ago? Well, she was messing with Tommy off and on even though she had a man."

Michelle jumped in and said, "That's Tommy for you!" then frowned and leaned on the wall.

Natalia swallowed and tapped her feet on the linoleum floor with rage in her eyes. She couldn't believe that I was still messing with Tommy after hearing all the horror stories on how he treated women. "So why did you lie to me, Missy?" She stood waiting for an answer.

"What did she lie about?" Michelle asked.

I sat up and said, "About six months ago, I told her that we were not an item anymore."

"Why?" Daddy asked.

"I didn't want her to continue the normal routine, worrying about me."

Stretching her arms out while still trying to remain calm, she said, "Well, it sounds as if everyone knew you was still with him but me. Why is that?" She rolled her eyes in disgust.

"Didn't I just say that I didn't want you to worry?" I spat back as I slumped down.

Daddy looked exhausted. But he still wasn't finished being the Herald Sun newspaper for the day. "Yeah, Lola's baby's daddy got a hold of that boy and shot him six good times. Too bad he didn't kill him."

"Daddy!" I shouted.

Michelle didn't take lightly that I was being ganged up on. "Okay, Pastor Jones, you really need to repent for that comment," she said as she held her forehead.

Daddy looked over at me as if he could see through my brain. "Gal, you better be glad I didn't pull the trigger. He needs a good whoopin'. Maybe if we beat on him a little, he will stop beating on you." Everyone became so quiet that you could hear a pin drop. Natalia held onto the chair and leaned back in shock.

"Okay, I think I'm about to pop off. Let me get this straight. Someone came to the church house and shot the man with Missy in the room?"

"Yes, Lord, in the church house, in my study. I've been preaching at Mt. Zion for fifteen years and I ain't never seen someone that bold. But these children today don't care about nothing."

"Church just ain't a sacred place anymore," Natalia said.

Michelle put her head down and started praying as she seemed really emotional during the entire conversation. I could tell that she did not want Natalia getting all animated, upsetting me even more. Natalia put her hand on her hip and nodded her head as if she were in deep thought. "So, the question of the day is, when do we bury that nut?"

Daddy laughed. "The devil doesn't go down that easily, gal. We don't have that type of favor today, maybe tomorrow. That fool is still alive. Matter of fact, I hear he is in this here hospital on the eighth floor."

"I should go up there and pull all the plugs out of the wall," Michelle said as she grabbed at the air.

I stared at Michelle. "Girl, you okay?"

"No, I am not. But I will be all right. Give me a minute," she replied as she fanned herself with her hand.

"I feel your pain, Michelle. I want to do that, too, but the way my daughter is looking right now, I will tend to him later."

"I know that's right," Natalia said.

"I wish you all would stop making such a big deal out of this. Everyone is okay and life will move on. I will be back at the pulpit in no time. I have had these anxiety breakdowns before. No big deal." I tried really hard to ease everyone's mind. I knew I probably looked helpless lying in this bed and I didn't want to keep talking about Tommy. Especially since I hadn't even laid eyes on him since the shooting.

"Lord, girl, when you gonna let that man go? He is the cause of these breakdowns you know." Natalia shook her head as she put her hand on my shoulder.

I pulled my shoulder away, angered by the group therapy. "I will be all right. I don't need this intervention. It's all a part of God's plan. We will get through this."

Daddy put both hands over his face in shame. He looked drained. "I hope so, baby girl, I hope so. I just pray we don't see you on the next episode of *Snapped*. I'm getting ready to go home and lay down. I'm too old for all this drama." As he looked up to the ceiling, he shouted, "Lord, give her strength to move on. Jesus, I just need you to take the wheel."

Chapter 7

Two weeks later....

Sunday morning arrived, and it was time for Family and Friends day at Mt. Zion Holiness Church. The church members were ready to give a high praise to the Lord for His goodness and mercy. The older saints brought family members from near and far to hear me preach. I would always open up the service with a song to get the crowd pumped before bringing the word.

"Amazing Grace, how sweeeeet the sound…that saved a wretch like meeeeeee."

I saw some of the congregation close their eyes to savor the sweet experience of reaching God's presence. Singing was always an essential part of the service. My daddy told me at an early age that singing was a good step ladder into a sinner's heart.

"Jesus, thank you, Jesus! Sing, child, sing!" Mother Smithfield yelled as she raised her right hand to God and moved her elbow up and down. She was our oldest member and enjoyed listening to me sing. Although, she was not a pleasant person to be around, we loved her anyway. She tried hard to play the role of being one of the most supportive mothers in the church, but it didn't always work.

THAT CHURCH LIFE

"Hallelujah," yelled Mother Gaines who sat right beside Mother Smithfield every Sunday, no matter what.

I had to close my eyes each time I blurted out a note due to the pain I felt inside. My emotions ran high as I thought about Tommy still being in the hospital fighting for his life. I didn't have the courage to go and see him. I couldn't handle the sight of breathing tubes, machines and IV's that were probably hanging all around him. I tried hard to erase each thought of his condition and allowed the sorrow to come out in my facial expression while singing.

The congregation was not concerned with my countenance as they all nodded while my solo helped them to reach heaven. The expressions on each face signified that they had that "good feeling" that poured all over their bodies from a higher spiritual entity.

"Lord, I hear you! Lord, I hear you! Hallelujah!" Mother Gaines yelled again.

The old church members called this good feeling the "Holy Ghost" and it was an indescribable excitation that you couldn't shake nor run from.

I finished my song and was ready to preach the word. I stepped closer to the podium and put my head down to pray. "Father God, I come to you as humbly as I know how. I am asking that as you increase, I decrease as I bring forth your word to your people. Allow them to hear all that you have to say in Jesus' name, Amen."

"Amen."

I grabbed my blue laced handkerchief that was placed in my bible and used it to rub my forehead. I wanted to be oil free as the lights and cameras shined brightly in my face. Even so, my make-up dripped onto my collar while I used my index finger to wipe it away.

The congregation listened attentively as I began.

"There is so much confusion in this world. Can I talk about it today, church?"

"Yes, you can. Preach, daughter."

My daddy was glad to get a break from the pulpit. He loved to sit and watch me work the audience.

My stepmother, who I really didn't care for, sat on the other side of him facing the congregation. She supported me as much as she knew how. The title of "First Lady" went straight to her head after only a few years of being married. She had a habit of blinking her fake eyelashes while smiling with a half grin.

I looked over quickly at her big brimmed purple hat. Tonya Jones was her name and taking all of Daddy's money was her game. She couldn't compare to my graceful submissive mother. May God rest her soul.

I moved, turning to my dad, holding the microphone up high as he looked alert and vibrant. He appeared giddy as he shuffled his feet, becoming excited before I could give the congregation the scripture.

"Turn to Matthew twenty, verse four."

THAT CHURCH LIFE

The congregation scuffled through their bibles searching for the verse on cell phones and hard copy. The big screen behind me also showed each verse with a yellow tint of color.

"Let us all stand and read God's word."

We read it in unison and when the reading was complete, everyone sat back down in their plush blue cushioned seats.

"This verse talks about Jesus sending folks into the vineyard to do some work in order to get what's owed to them. The next in line thought they should have received more than the last."

"Come on with it, gal!" Daddy shouted.

"The bible says that many are called, but few are chosen to really do the work required in the vineyard. Church, I encourage you today to get busy and do the work that the Lord is expecting you to do. Don't let the things of this world distract you. Can I get a witness?"

"Well, say it again, sister!" a woman in the front row shouted.

I pulled the microphone closer to my chest and tilted my head forward. "Just like David in Psalms, we got to go through some stuff to get what is due. The first group in line had to go through several hours of walking back and forth and still didn't get what they thought they should have. But it wasn't up to them to make that decision. Who are they to say what they should get? They are workers. Workers do the work and ask questions later."

"Well!" Mother Smithfield said.

"The vineyard needs a few good women and men. Are you ready, church?"

Daddy moved his head to the side with his black handkerchief high in the air and shouted, "And it is so, daughter! Do the work, church. Do the work!"

I continued as sweat dripped down my neck. "Don't let fear and doubt stop you from doing the work. You see, God does not give us the spirit of fear but of power and of love and of a sound mind. We can't keep walking around here worrying about every situation and what is due to us. We have to put it in His hands."

I looked over at the organ, forgetting that Tommy was not there. By this time into a sermon, our eyes would meet, and he would give me a wink to let me know that I was giving a good word.

I looked down at the floor to gain focus, realizing that I was going into another daydreaming trance. Of course, physically he would not be here. Spiritually, it was as if I felt his soft tender lips touch my cheek.

I wiped my nose with my handkerchief and said, "Whoa, Jesus, help us, Lord!"

"Yes, yes, yes, help us, Lord!" Mother Gaines stood up shouting.

I became teary-eyed as the cameras zoomed in on me standing behind the pulpit. I was sure they thought it was the word that brought me to tears again. I wouldn't give them the satisfaction of knowing otherwise. "God will see us through it all, church, but we got to get to work in His vineyard to prepare others for His kingdom."

"Amen."

Michelle was on the organ prepping her hands to start. The music started to come in softly in the background as I continued. "We will get through the rough days and the sunshine will come out again. Lead me to the rock that is higher than I, Lord. Lead me to the victory. Lead me to peace and allow me to do the work that is needed. Amen!"

"Amen!" the church said in unison.

Mother Gaines became really happy and started bouncing her shoulders up and down. The Holy Spirit got her before I could finish saying everything I had written down on paper. She was riled up and couldn't decide if she wanted to scoot her wide butt across the pew in slow motion or just plop in the middle of the floor with her eyes looking toward the sky.

"Yes, sweet baby Jesus! Lead me, Lord. Lead me!" Mother Gaines reached a higher spiritual realm than anyone else in the service. She carried on as if she had suppressed spiritual emotions that could only come out at that moment.

The ushers walked up to her pew, dressed in their black suits, white gloves, and white crisply starched shirts. They carried a cardboard fan with a funeral home advertisement on one side and used it to fan her back into reality.

"Oh glory. Yes, Lord. Oh my, my, my," she screamed, slumping over on her side as if an invisible someone was abusing her. Something that looked so harsh and harmful seemed to feel better than a Bengay rub for such an old, energetic and feisty woman.

"Yeah, God, I see you working it out!" Daddy yelled as he looked over at her and reached his arms toward heaven.

Mother Smithfield was irritated by Mother Gain's performance as she held up the service. Mother Smithfield whispered, but could still be heard, "Sit your old butt down before you fall and hurt yourself, woman."

Mother Gaines sat straight up and opened her eyes from her hypnotic spell as her flowered dress flitted up in the air showing her undergarments. She turned to her pew partner and said, "Smithfield, why do you bother to come to church, huh?"

"Because I want to," she hissed.

"I'm trying to praise God and you are breaking my spirit."

"And the Oscar goes to... You will be all right, child," Mother Smithfield snickered.

Mother Gaines pointed, shaking her finger in front of her face. "You been going here for thirty years and still ain't saved!"

"You better hush!" Mother Smithfield demanded.

"Now you know God ain't pleased with that, nah uh, not one bit. Whoa glory, help her, God!"

Mother Smithfield balled up her fist, edging closer, lining up her body hip to hip and said, "You might want to stop talking to me, child. You don't want these paws on you, now do you, my dear?"

Mother Gaines shoved her fist down to her side. "The day you put your old hands on me is the day you are going home to glory," she countered, rolling her eyes. Sinking deep into her seat, Mother Gaines stopped her praise and shut down, sitting still like a child that was just chastised by its mother.

Mother Smithfield became disoriented and couldn't focus, she had to get the last word in to end it. "I rebuke that spirit, Lord. In the name of Jesus. Shundo!"

I tried to finish giving the rest of my sermon without laughing. I was hoping the cameras didn't catch all the action. My tired limbs began to quiver while I stood leaning onto the podium. It became obvious that I was not fully recovered from my previous attack. I tried to play it all off but remained weak. Daddy flapped his hands in the air, stomped a foot and tilted his head back in praise.

I ended with, "Think on these things."

Before the service could continue, Daddy had to give follow-up remarks. He skipped to the microphone and grabbed it like he was James Brown singing, "Baby please don't go." He looked around the congregation and paused for a few seconds in silence as the cameras re-centered. His thick beard and wide nose moved from side to side as he spoke loudly in holy tongue.

He gained composure and said, "Lord knows that was a good word for my soul. Didn't she preach, church?" he asked as he looked around for confirmation. "I said, didn't she preach, church?"

"Amen!"

"All right, now get your money out of your pockets and let's take up our offering and tithes. Now don't hold back on God. Give him what He asked for. Amen?"

"Amen."

Each member reached deep into their pockets and purses looking for money to put into the straw baskets that were held up high in the air by the four ushers. The pulpit members with all of the clergy were the first group to walk around the altar.

I wasn't up to giving the last words and final benediction so instead of walking back to my seat, I walked toward the front door. Daddy took over and gave positive words as the music played loudly. Each member rotated throughout the long aisles walking closer to the basket. They looped around and migrated back to their seats.

Daddy called for a prayer line after the last person dropped their money into the black hole of church commerce. This was a perfect time to exit.

I walked down the middle aisle with minimal eye contact. I looked straight ahead, walking toward the front door, not wanting to greet anyone. Before I could make it completely down the church stairway, I was stopped dead in my tracks in my high-heeled stilettos.

Chapter 8

At the bottom of the steps, I spotted a woman standing in the middle of the parking lot. She was frail, light skinned, skinny with long curly hair. She wore a black dress with a belt around her almost nonexistent waist. Her feet were tiny and looked as if she could wear a size six from the little girl's shoe section. She had her hand on her hip as she spoke loudly on her black, flip cell phone.

She turned in my direction and looked surprised to see me. "Joe, let me call you back; she is here, alone."

I looked around to see if there was anyone behind me. No way could she be talking about me. I didn't recall laying eyes on this strange looking woman in all my days. She walked with a slow stride as she came closer to the stairs. I reached for my pepper spray tucked in my Coach bag, not knowing what to expect. After all, this was the "Bull City" and I didn't want to take any chances of getting harmed by a stranger. Not knowing her intentions, I stepped back with hesitation.

I was afraid of her possibly being one of Tommy's *special* friends. I was not in the mood for more drama, but just like the devil, he would always show up after I preached a good and heartfelt sermon. She glared at me for over thirty seconds and then spoke with a low soft tone. "Is that you? Is it really you, Missy?"

Still looking around, I was trying to figure out who this person was as I held my pepper spray above my thirty-eight, double D chest. "Have we met?"

"Isn't your name Missy Jones?"

I took the cap off my pepper spray, leaning into a ninja stance ready to aim, shoot and fire. "Who wants to know?"

She wiped the sweat off her forehead and walked closer, invading my personal space. "I have been wanting to see you since the very first day they took you away from me."

With my hand over my mouth, I was frustrated with the vague statement. "Excuse me?"

Her eyes filled with large droplets as she tucked her face away in her hands. "Thank you, Jesus. Thank God you're okay. I'm sorry, my name is Olivia... Olivia Wallace."

Still uncertain as to why I should care about a woman named Olivia Wallace, I said, "How can I help you, Olivia? Are you one of Tommy's friends?"

She twisted her lips to the side. "I don't know who you're referring to, but I drove three days just to see your pretty sweet face. I knew the day you were born that you would grow up to be a beautiful and intelligent young lady."

I scratched my head, looking down at the ground with my face wrinkled. "You drove three days to see me? I'm sorry, but I can't say that I have ever met you before. Are you an old member?"

She reached into her purse and fumbled through papers. "I want you to take a look at this. I'm not here to hurt you, so you can put away your spray, lady."

"I'm not putting my spray away until you tell me what this is all about." I looked down at the photo she had pulled out. I stared at the picture for a moment before I said, "The only thing I see is a lady holding a baby, and that lady resembles you. Is that you, ma'am?"

She smiled with glistening eyes. "Yes, that is me. The baby that I'm holding is you, my dear child. My one and only."

"Wait, your one and only what?" I put my hand on my neck and looked around, scanning the parking lot. "Are you an old friend of the family or something? How in the world could you be holding me in this picture? Ma'am, you need to give more details. You're making me nervous."

"You don't know me because your daddy doesn't want you to know me," the woman said, scratching her arms.

A woman I had never laid eyes on before was holding a picture of me as a baby and was saying that my daddy kept secrets. Never! "Lord God, what is really going on here!" I asked as I became impatient with the entire unexpected meet and greet.

The woman then pulled out a North Carolina birth certificate. "Read this, sweetie, and maybe you will understand."

I read the green piece of paper with words that looked like they came from an old-fashioned typewriter. I wanted to read it all out loud so that there would be no misunderstandings. "The living birth certificate of baby girl Missy Rochelle Jones."

It was written and signed by Lincoln Memorial Hospital in the city of Durham, North Carolina. "Parents are Henry Jones and Olivia Wallace." I leered at the woman and dropped the piece of paper out of my hands onto the cold ground. "You're my mother? No, no, no this can't be real. My real mother is Sylvia and she died of cancer when I was in middle school!"

I bent over holding my stomach looking around. Pain shot from my abdomen all the way up to my left temple. I was so not ready to get news like this, not now. I would have preferred her being one of Tommy's playmates than to be standing here proclaiming motherhood.

"The lady who raised you was my niece. I met your father in Goldsboro at a Holy Convention in 1988. He was a young minister, fresh out of high school and had a lot of potential. I really believed he loved me, but he was immature and made some very bad choices back then." She paused to catch her breath. "You see, Henry was stalked, craved, and desired by the entire church of hot and bothered women. They tried anything and everything to take him away from me. Young, old, fat, skinny, it didn't matter, he was a hot commodity back then."

I stopped her in the middle of her insane story that broke the camel's back and asked, "Wait, so you're saying the lady that I believed to be my mother all of my life is your niece?"

I couldn't believe what I was hearing. This had to be a joke. I knew there were some cameras hidden somewhere in the bushes. Within twenty seconds, my friends would jump out and say, "Surprise!" This wasn't happening. Not at a time such as this. I was already an anxiety train wreck.

"Yes, my niece. We were only a few years apart. I was the youngest of my siblings and she was the daughter of my oldest sister. She lived with me while she was growing up for a few years when her mother moved to Boston for work. Your dad and I moved to Durham shortly after we met to get away from all the madness in Goldsboro." She paused again to see my reaction. "My niece moved in with us until she could get on her own two feet. I gave her a place to stay, food to eat and even helped her get a job down at the Liggett & Myers tobacco company. I always came to her rescue and never dreamed that she would sleep with my man while I was at work and run off with him and my child into the sunset."

I felt like I could have died and gone to heaven right then and there. "Wow, this sounds like a bad reality show. Why haven't you come to find me before now?"

She admittedly said, "I am so sorry that you didn't know about me, but I'm sure Mr. Jones didn't want his church reputation tarnished. He didn't want church folks to know that he made a baby out of wedlock. I wanted to come and get you a few times but I couldn't break the deal I made with him. He would make it really hard for me if I didn't stay away."

I was startled by her comment. "Ms. Olivia, you're making this up. My mom was a saint."

She chuckled. It seemed to make her feel good to tell me information that would make my father look like the Tasmanian devil. "I know it all sounds crazy, but it's the truth. I left the state when Sylvia became terminally ill. I asked for a job transfer because I couldn't stay in North Carolina anymore not being able to see you and I never looked back. It was hard to save money for such a long trip back to Durham. But this time I took a chance and borrowed money from friends to get here from California. I felt empty when I got the call from my brother of your disappearance. I didn't want another day to pass by without seeing your pretty face."

I wrinkled my face with concern. "Are you kidding me? Never in a million years would I have dreamed that Sylvia Shanice Jones was not my biological mother!"

I stared at the woman in front of me and admired Olivia's strong features which I began to see that I also carried. She had beautiful gleaming big eyes that were the centerpiece of her sculpted face that resembled someone from Indian descent, and now I knew why I had such long legs. "I don't know what else to say, Ms. Olivia. My dad has never said anything bad about your niece and he never let on that she wasn't my mother. I know this is a messed-up situation, but I want you to know she took really good care of me."

She flung back her hair looking vexed. "I'm sure she did, sweetie. She didn't have a choice. That was the deal we made when they took you from me. She had to make a vow to take great care of you for such a huge sacrifice. I know I wasn't ready for a child but he didn't even want to give me a chance. With practice, I could have made a great mother. I will give her some credit, she did allow me to see you from time to time. She would put you in her red Ford pickup truck and drive you down Hwy 40 East to Goldsboro some Sundays after church, just to visit me. Of course, your daddy didn't know anything about our meetings."

"Why would you agree to this? Why would you do this to your seed?" I asked. Olivia looked like she was peeping into an hourglass as she recounted her past. She seemed angry at herself as if she wanted to rescind all of her previous decisions and start over again. She pulled out another picture.

"Your dad seemed to think that his ancient secret was safe, especially once his mother died. Little does he know that it was leaked to a few of the older church members who are probably still members of Mt. Zion. I'm sure someone here can verify that I am telling the truth."

"I haven't heard a thing from anyone about you," I said, still looking dumbfounded.

"His mama trusted a few folks and I'm sure she shared it with at least one true friend."

"I'm sure she did. But I bet they were all sworn to secrecy until their last day of life; they worshiped the ground my grandmother walked on. I guess they all kept their word since I haven't heard about it."

Olivia rubbed her arm as she put her head down. "Yeah, they loved Pastor Jones. They wouldn't do that to her."

Thinking positive, I said, "Well, all that doesn't matter now, Ms. Olivia. What matters is you had the courage to come and see about me." I tried to seem happy and formulate a fake grin, but based upon her uneasy wrinkled facial expressions, it wasn't working. It was obvious that she was picking up on how I really felt.

She reached out to touch my face. "When my brother saw you on the news a week ago, he called me right away. He said it was as if he was looking at the spitting image of me. I became so worried about you, my heart ached for days. All I could think about was someone hurting you due to your daddy's past. The news never reported why that man came in shooting."

I looked up at the stairway, ignoring the sentimental moment, worried that service would be ending any minute now. "Well, we can talk some other time in another location, can't we? I'm sure after Daddy finishes with the altar call, he will be dismissing service and it won't be a pretty scene if he sees you."

She seemed sad. "Okay, I understand. May I hug you, Missy Jones?"

"Um." I felt so uncomfortable and cringed. "Yes, I guess that would be nice."

She embraced me tightly, rocking me back and forth, and then gave me a piece of paper with all of her contact information. "It was a pleasure seeing your pretty face, Missy Jones. I guess it's see you next time? Until we meet again?"

"I guess," I responded.

"Please, let's be in touch. I would love to share more over lunch," she said with enthusiasm.

My eyes were worn out due to several weeks of crying worrying about Tommy and still filled with anxiety. She became a big blurry fragment standing in front of me. All I could do was close them tightly, hoping for a second of relief as the wind shifted, creating a burning sensation as we hugged. It felt as if a storm was underway.

"Yes, until we meet again. God Bless."

I walked across the parking lot and didn't look back. I couldn't believe this was happening and I wished I could erase the entire conversation out of my head. I got in my car and hit my head on the steering wheel several times. When it rains, it pours. My stress level was unreal, and I didn't know how many more curve balls from life I could possibly take. My heart was filled with pain as I ran the palm of my hand around my furry, Panther's, turquoise and black, steering wheel cover.

How dare my daddy not tell me about my biological mother? He allowed me to go my entire life without knowing the truth. I wiped my eyes, clearing away the residue from my tears in order to see the road in front of me. I buckled my seatbelt and sucked in my gut, then I drove away as fast as my Nissan would allow.

Chapter 9

After leaving the church parking lot in a daze, I remained distraught. The image of two loving parents who were painted so pretty and bright was not really my life. All this time I worried about how the church viewed me while trying hard not to embarrass my family. However, to hear that my father was not the perfect man that I cherished but was a man who had so many secrets in his past life was almost blasphemous. Mom, a man stealer? Oh wait, not really my mom, but cousin? Stuff like this makes me want to cuss.

I turned on the radio and began to listen to The Light 103.9, trying to channel out the madness. The song, "In the Middle" came on and I turned up the volume in an attempt to drown my thoughts. God sure does have a sense of humor!

The song spoke to me, letting me know that I was surely in the middle of some mess, but God was in the middle right along with me. After hearing all that nonsense, I decided my track record of having bad relationships was better than creating out-of-wedlock babies and then, taking newborns from their mothers. The wish factor played in my head along with the beat. I wish someone would say something about me being in love with Tommy Davis!

I drove down the Durham Freeway heading in the direction of Duke Hospital. I was now determined more than ever to see him. With my lead foot on the gas pedal, I pushed the speed up to eighty miles per hour. I was so frustrated that I didn't even think about my chances of getting another speeding ticket.

I knew Tommy was probably still on the eighth floor in ICU, fighting to live just for me. I prayed while swerving around the highway curves that he was coherent and would be able to recognize me. I missed his jokes, his smile, his laugh and his touch, his everything.

I arrived at the hospital in no time and pulled up to the valet parking section.

"How can I help you, ma'am?" the attendant asked, wearing a white collared shirt and white gloves covering his big hands.

"Can you please park my car closer to the front of the hospital, sir? I'm sure it will be late when I leave out so for safety reasons."

"Well, for a pretty lady like you, I can do that. I got you covered," he said as he winked at me. I winked back to seal the deal—a little flirting to ensure that he did just as I said.

I jumped out of my Nissan Maxima and handed the keys over to the attendant. I looked up and down, assessing all of the floors of the huge monumental hospital. I walked carefully through the revolving doors while my three-inch heels had difficulty gripping the slippery linoleum floor. My heels clanked against the tiles on my way to the elevator.

"What floor are you going to, ma'am," a man dressed in hospital scrubs asked.

"Can you please press number eight?" Looking down at my feet, I wiggled my legs and repositioned my feet. I didn't want to lose my heel tips after walking fast while trying to balance in my shoes.

The elevator moved up, inching its way to the ICU area. A bell sounded at each floor. I reached the eighth floor and heard a computerized voice say, "Going up."

I got off the elevator and walked straight to the front desk. "Hi, I am looking for Tommy Lee Davis. Is he still an ICU patient here?" The nurse looked me up and down, puzzled, it seemed, by my attire.

"You look like you're on your way to a prom, Ms. Thang with that long silk dress hitting the floor," she smirked as she looked for his name.

"No, I'm too old for a prom. I just left a church service."

"If you dress like that for church, what does your Christmas party outfit look like?"

I chuckled at her little joke, not knowing if she was giving me a compliment or an insult. I tapped my heel becoming impatient with the small talk and nodded. "I guess I will take that as a compliment."

She smiled as she continued to read Tommy's chart. "It says here that I can't let anyone in who isn't a spouse or family member."

"Well, he doesn't have any family here in North Carolina and he isn't married."

"I don't know about that, sugah. His wife came up here earlier to sign consent forms for surgery." She looked at me with a smug look as she probably put two and two together thinking that I was the side chick.

"There is definitely an impostor signing his documents then."

She didn't budge and continued to stare.

"I'm his cousin. Let him know that I'm here to see him."

She looked down again at the list. "Yeah, okay, cousin. What's your name, hun?"

Standing at attention, I said, "Missy Jones."

"Oh, I think I have heard your name around town. Are you related to that pastor with the mega church on PBS television station?"

"Yes, he's my father."

"Oh nice! Preacher's kid! Ms. Jones, sorry to inform you, but your name is not on the list as a family member. Sorry."

"Well, can I call him then?"

"Sure, you can call him anytime at extension 5542. But I would wait until tomorrow, he's heavily sedated today. Then again, you don't want the wife answering either," she said with sarcasm.

I became irate instantly and stomped my left foot, almost breaking my heel again. "Look here, lady. You don't have a clue on what you're talking about. Tommy is not married and you are being very disrespectful right now. The Lord doesn't appreciate you acting ugly to one of His most anointed vessels. So, stop playing with my emotions and tell me when I can come back to see my man?"

She chuckled loudly, pointing at my temper tantrum and said, "Oh, now he's your man? Honey, you gonna learn to do a background check the next time you date someone. From the looks of this paperwork, he don't belong to you, so please leave with your nasty acting, holier than thou attitude before I call security."

The nurse walked away and waved her middle finger in the air as if she was giving me the shoo fly signal. She yelled, "Sanctified folks are so ridiculous!"

I stood quietly, still tapping my foot and drumming my fingers on the desk. I took two deep breaths before walking away. I had been dating Tommy on and off for over four years. When did he have time to get married on me? There was no way he could be married.

As I walked slowly to the elevator, I created an imaginary timeline in my head. Without hesitation, I reached the ground floor, opened my cell phone and the main hospital number to be transferred to Tommy's room.

"Hello?"

"Tommy?"

"Yes, who is this?"

I scratched my head. "Don't play with me, honey. You know who this is."

Loud laughter came through the phone. "This isn't Tommy. This is his brother, Arnold." For some reason he thought his prank was funny. "Is this Amy?"

My heart sank as my face turned red thinking about a possible wife. "Amy? No, my name is…wait, who is Amy?"

"Oh, I'm sorry. I thought this was Amy, the internal medicine doctor. Who is this?"

"Missy."

"Oh Yeah, I've heard your name before. Tommy has spoken highly of you."

I felt relieved. I knew the story of Tommy having a wife couldn't possibly be true. "Glad to hear he had nice things to say about me. Is he able to talk right now?"

"No, not at this time," he said.

"I will try back in a few days if that's okay."

"That will be fine. Tommy is still not in any condition to talk to anyone over the phone. He's running a fever and it might be at least a week before he will be able to receive visitation."

"I understand," I said.

"My wife and I are taking turns monitoring his progress so one of us should be here. I'm sure he would love to see you, so stop by as well."

I smiled. His wife? Thank you, Jesus! So, it's *his* wife that is signing the consent forms.

"Well, thanks for the update."

"You're welcome. Just know that he's coming along just fine. Ask for me the next time you stop by and I will try to sneak you in. I know the nurse at the front can be a tough one. We wanted to make sure that only close family could visit for security purposes, you know? The shooter has not been caught yet."

"I understand."

"I will also try to put your name on the list as family next time as well."

I sighed. "That sounds great." I was happy that his brother acknowledged me as someone special in his life. "Hug him for me. I'll catch up with you in a few days."

I hung up and could now head home feeling happy about something positive.

THAT CHURCH LIFE

Chapter 10

It was 7:00 a.m. and my alarm clock startled me. Twinkles perked his head up at me for a few seconds, trying to figure out what all the noise was about and then laid back down. I had to get back into a routine and go back to work. I jumped out of bed rubbing Twinkles on his head and feeling better about Tommy's situation. I gleamed at the fact that he was making progress and would soon be lying in his arms. I wasn't going to share with anyone about my mother's visit or my attempt to visit Tommy except for Michelle. Michelle could hold information for decades. Natalia, on the other hand, couldn't hold a bottle of water steady, much less private information. I didn't want to hear the sarcasm from Natalia, nor did I want the continued judgment.

I walked into the bathroom to shower with my head bonnet still tightly in place and my fuzzy pink socks gliding on the hardwood floors. The phone rang, and I dashed back onto my bed to pick it up before it went to voicemail.

"Hello."

"Hey, girly. I just called to see if you were going back to work today. How are you?" Natalia was an early riser and sounded as if she had been up for hours, full of energy.

"Yes, to remain sane I don't have a choice, hun. Sitting around the house another week is not going to help my situation."

"That is true, dear, but I was thinking maybe I could help you forget all your troubles by taking you far away from Durham for a little vacation."

Feeling hopeful about having an opportunity to get away from all the madness, I answered, "Where, when and how long?"

"Well, we can fly out to Jamaica for some good ole sunshine and rest. I can invite Michelle and we'll make it a girlfriend's trip. What do you say?"

"Yes, that would be great!" I knew a relaxing Caribbean vacation might be a good thing for me. I called to check on Tommy and his brother told me he wasn't coherent due to the new medications. He was now down to just his brother as a visitor, so this was perfect timing to sneak away for a trip.

"I'll call Michelle to see if she's able to take off work and then I will make the arrangements. We can leave as early as tomorrow if that's okay with you?"

"Fantastic! Tomorrow? That's a fast turnaround, but I can't refuse a free trip, so let's do it! Let me check with my job to make sure it's okay. I will tell them I need another week off to recoup!" I sat on the edge of my king-size bed playing with the frilly strings on my blanket.

"Yeah, I'm hoping this trip will allow you to take some weight off your shoulders. You have been carrying everyone's burdens with all this worry and frustration about the church and what people think. Now it's time for you to take care of you. So, let's do this." Natalia began to sing Bob Marley's song, "Jamming" in her falsetto.

"Girl, hang this phone up. No one wants to hear bird calls this early in the morning!"

Natalia chuckled. "Well, I know I can't sing as good as you, but I am sure after you have a few of those Jamaican Smile drinks, you will bird chirp just like me."

"Girl, you are crazy. Get the information and call me back with the flight info. I need to start packing!"

"I know that's right. Make sure you have some booty shorts and a two-piece bathing suit ready."

"I'm a minister. I will not be a hoochie while in another country."

She paused. "Girl, you will be in a place where no one knows your silly church title, nor will they care. You got to let the title thing go while we are there and let loose. You might find a Jamaican Tyrone to bring back home with you."

"See, you are too much, Lord have mercy. Why can't it be a Jamaican Tony or Mark?"

"Everything goes over your head. The song, 'Call Tyrone' that Erica Badu sings… Never mind!"

"Talk to you later, girl. The last thing I need is a Jamaican Tyrone in my life. Maybe a Caleb, but not Tyrone."

"Well, you never know who the Lord has for you. Later, sweets."

Going on a trip? Yes, Lord! I had a boss who was understanding and didn't mind when I took random vacations. At Research Triangle Engineering, the vacation and sick benefits were flexible and layered with options. It worked well with my lifestyle. I had been a project manager for over eight years and I was proud to be with such a prestigious company. I took off quite often to attend convocations and revivals while preaching around the state. I had over sixty days of vacation time saved after working all these years, so it was never a problem.

I put the house phone to my ear, listening for a dial tone and began to dial my work number. "Good morning! I would like to speak to Mr. Holloway, please."

His secretary knew my voice instantly and responded with enthusiasm. "Good morning, Ms. Jones! I'll transfer you right over."

I heard a clicking noise and a voice came through within seconds.

"Good morning, this is Mr. Holloway."

"Good morning, Mr. Holloway, this is Missy Jones."

"Hello, Missy! How you feelin'?"

"I'm calling to tell you that I will need another week off from work. I'm still not fully recovered from my illness, so I think it's best that I take additional time to recuperate."

He paused. "That's totally understandable, Missy. Please take all the time you need. I'll have Stacy handle all of your projects until you return."

"That would be great, sir. Thank you for allowing me to do this on such short notice."

"No problem at all. We all need a break every now and again."

"Great! Thanks for everything and hopefully I will see you next week. Please tell Ms. Stacy I said thank you for covering for me."

"I sure will. Take care now."

"Thanks again. Goodbye."

I put the phone back on the hook, taking a deep breath while thinking about the variety of sun dresses in my dress collection that would be perfect for an island trip. *Finally!* Traveling outside of North Carolina was truly a treat. This trip was right on time due to my trial and error with new anxiety pills.

I glanced at the piece of paper my "new" mother had given to me; it sat next to the phone. I contemplated on when I should call her to chat. After staring at the phone for a few minutes, I picked it up to call her. It went straight to voicemail. I was disappointed that my dad kept this information to himself after all these years. But I was even more disappointed that my grandmother gave information to someone in the church. I wondered who that person could be and if they were still living. I was sure it was probably one of the older saints who always seemed to give me a hard time. I bet Mother Smithfield knew something.

Hearing her version before talking to my father might be helpful. I needed to know something before I left the country. She would get right to the point whereas my dad would take days to give me every detail. It was certain that if anyone knew something, it would be her. She knew everyone and everything from Durham to Richmond, Virginia.

After taking a shower and putting on clothes, I figured maybe visiting Mother Smithfield should be sooner rather than later. Blue Manor nursing home was only ten minutes away from my house. I could make an appearance and come right back to pack.

Without thinking about it any longer, I picked up Twinkles and raced down the stairs. I knocked on my neighbor's door, explaining my situation of leaving for vacation so that my cat could have a sitter while I was away.

With a brisk walk to the parking lot, I hopped into my car on a mission. I anticipated getting all of the missing pieces to my life's puzzle from dear old Mother Smithfield.

THAT CHURCH LIFE

Chapter 11

Mother Shirley Smithfield was petite and dark with a head full of gray hair. She wore flowered long dresses that always seemed to match her hat and shoes. She never married, but she'd had seven children by the same man. He left her when the last child turned three. Through the years of being alone with seven children, she seemed bitter, but tried really hard to smile anyhow, especially around church folk. She made a vow to the Lord at an early age that Mt. Zion would be the only church she attended during her lifetime.

I remember the ole days when she picked me up on weekends to play with her children. Because of her devotion to my grandmother, she did everything she could to help me. Not having siblings made it easy for her to take me in as one of her own. She was adamant about teaching bible verses, hymns and how to cook good ole sweet potato pie.

I grew older and she started coming by less and less. I guess after hitting a certain age, she no longer felt needed. It didn't matter, I knew she loved me even when she didn't show it. I was sure if she knew anything about my father's past, she wouldn't have a problem with telling the God's honest truth.

I entered the nursing home expecting to find Mother Smithfield in her room watching television. Instead, I caught her in the dining hall area playing her favorite past time, bingo.

"Look who came in to see little old me. Missy Jones! What did I do to deserve this visit, chile?" She smiled looking down at my shoes.

I leaned over to hug her. "Oh stop it, Mother Smithfield. You know that I always try to come and see you when I'm in this part of town."

She chuckled. "Yeah, you must love me or something." She was known for telling the truth that would sometimes hurt the feelings of others but she had a good heart and that was all that mattered.

I smiled and said, "Yes, I sure do love you, Mother. More than you realize."

"What brings you to these parts of the railroad track?"

"I wanted to talk to you about my father."

Her eyebrows arched unintentionally as she looked away to see who else was listening. "What about your father?" she whispered.

"Someone came to visit me after I left church on Sunday and it was a real eerie surprise."

She threw down her bingo chip and looked up. "Chile, talk a little lower if you don't want these folks in your business." She looked around the table. "Oh, and who was that?"

"Olivia," I whispered.

Without blinking or looking at me, she threw another bingo chip down. "I kind of figured she would pop up one day."

"Oh, so you know her?"

"Chile, you know I know all about her. Just wondered when she would show up."

"She didn't have anything nice to say about my dad. It seems that he was very loving to her niece whom I thought was my mother."

Her dark smooth skin became pale as she looked up and said, "That's a man for you. A man is only saved from the waist line up, ain't you learned that yet, chile?"

I began to sniffle thinking about all the deception. I had never known my dad to withhold information from me. It hurt to think about it as I wiped my nose trying not to cry in front of her. Mother Smithfield didn't go for a lot of crying. "So I guess no one was going to tell me about all of this, huh?"

"I told your grandmother right before she died that she needed to let the cat out of the bag so you could be free. She didn't think you were ready to hear it at that age."

The more we talked about my daddy's past, the harder she threw her bingo chips down on the table.

I looked at her with pleading eyes. "Please tell me all about my mother."

"Now you know I don't bite my tongue for no one, you know that," she said as she snickered, and reached out for my hand. "Are you really ready to hear the truth?"

"Yes, I know you will tell it like it is, so please, go right ahead." I looked over at her with a smirk.

"The entire Jones clan has always found trouble no matter how much they try to change with the Lord on their side."

I rolled my eyes, "So I've heard."

"Although they give off vibes of being perfect, there have been a lot of skeletons hidden in the church linen closet since I have been alive."

"Yes, I know that, too. Do tell," I replied as I prepared myself for the long speech.

"Now, your biological mama was wild and used to swing off them poles as young as seventeen years old. I don't think your daddy knew all of that when he started messing around with her."

My throat tightened and my eyes got big as my mind perked up to consume every detail of the story. "What kind of poles are you talking about, Mother?"

"Chile, you can't be that naïve! Don't you watch BET?"

I didn't know how to respond because I really didn't watch that channel. "Go ahead with your story, Mother."

"When he found out about her side hobbies outside the church house, he knew he couldn't marry her. Everyone knew he was next in line in becoming the pastor of Mt. Zion."

"I'm sure."

She grinned in delight, slapping her knee. "Chile, I've been itching to tell this story for twenty-seven years."

"Then why hold it this long? Especially considering that Grandma isn't here to stop you."

"I have to always honor the legacy of my good friend, Earline 'Big Mama' Jones. I sure do miss that woman," she said as her eyes dropped down.

An unidentified lady who sat across the table yelled, "You don't know nothing. You're an old coon that just loves to keep up mess."

Mother Smithfield yelled back, "Lee Lee, shut the hell up!" She then looked over at me and said, "Please excuse my language, lil' girl," then continued. "Now, you have known me for a long time. When have you ever known me to lie? And why you over here in my conversation?"

Lee Lee responded, "Can't help but to hear you. You loud and messy."

Mother frowned, sipping on her tall glass of sweet tea. She didn't appreciate Ms. Lee Lee Alston taking cheap shots and calling her out in front of company.

Lee Lee couldn't stop laughing as her round belly bumped the bingo table shaking all the bingo chips. Mother's facial expression said it all as she watched Lee Lee rubbing shoulders with the person sitting beside her.

"Look at her, pouting like a child."

The more she laughed, the more the table shook. Mother Smithfield cringed, holding her bingo chips close to her chest.

"Ignore her, Mother," I said as I watched her rage build.

It took all her might not to slide across the bingo table and smack the woman to the floor. She held her peace, listening to the announcer speak loudly into the microphone. He sat at the end of the table, spinning balls in a steel cage that spit out the numbers. Another number was called, "B12, going once, going twice. G59, going once, going twice."

Instantly, we heard, "I won, I won!" It was Ms. Lee Lee. She leaped into the air like a Harlem globetrotter making a winning shot. She jumped around the table waving her bingo card in everyone's faces as she trotted over to the prize table.

"Well now, it's definitely time to go!" Mother Smithfield packed her black sewing bag of goodies and headed out the door, holding her cane with a firm grip.

She said, "Come on, Missy, let's talk somewhere else. Ain't no privacy in this place full of ole folk."

Lee Lee knew by the looks of things she had pushed Mother Smithfield over the edge. "Wait, Shirley where you going?"

"Away from here, heifer! Can't even enjoy my visitor around your trifling self."

Lee Lee snickered as she picked out a coffee mug with Christmas tree drawings all around it. It looked as if a second grader made it for their dear old grandparent who donated it as a bingo gift. "This will be a perfect tea cup, won't it?" she said as she looked around the table, holding it up for confirmation.

I walked out with Mother, grabbing her bag and holding the middle of her free arm. We walked upstairs to her studio apartment within the independent living center.

She unlocked the door and spoke with a raspy tone, "In spite of what it looks like, Sylvia really loved you, girl. You meant the world to her. Olivia, however, didn't need no children. It was all God's plan. She ain't the saint she trying to portray to you, sugah. She was known for running off with other men and leaving you home with Sylvia. I bet she didn't tell you that part, huh?"

I stood in the middle of her room feeling disappointed. "Wow, no she didn't."

Mother looked away and said, "Shame on her."

I sat down at her kitchen table and crossed my legs, trying to process the new information. "But why now, why would she show up now?"

She sat in her recliner and rocked back and forth. "She's probably thinkin' you got some money or something to give her. Probably seen you on television preaching and saw nothing but dolla' signs."

"Why in the world would she think I have money?"

"That's been the word on the street for years, honey. I'm sure she is showing up wondering if you have access to an inheritance or somethin'."

I licked my lips. "I don't know anything about an inheritance, that's for sure."

"Either way, you have lived a good life without her. Don't let her minor disturbance bring you down. It ain't nothing but the devil."

"Thank you for talking to me, Mother. I surely appreciate the information." I reached over and gave her a long hug. I was grateful for her honesty and finally getting the truth.

"I am sure this truth will set you free, gal."

"I know it will. Thank you!"

I walked out holding onto my pink Coach purse tightly. I wanted to disown my father for holding onto such vital information. Regardless of being hurt and confused, I had a trip to get ready for.

Chapter 12

I returned home in a hurry. I had a lot to think about as I packed for the big trip. Six sundresses, ten pairs of underwear, three bras, two bathing suits and one pair of shorts were packed tightly in my mini pink Michael Kors suitcase. I was ready to create some positive memories with my girls.

I sat in my living room recliner waiting patiently with my bags in front of me. Each time a car passed by, I peeped out the window hoping to see Natalia's gold Jeep Cherokee outside. *Where are they?* I couldn't wait to get out of here.

A horn blew, and I knew that had to be my ride. I raced down the stairs with my suitcase bouncing off each step behind me. All I could think of was how good the food would be on the island. I imagined ordering a plate full of jerk chicken and curry goat as soon as I arrived at the resort. I had the pleasure of sampling authentic Jamaican food on Duke Street, but I was pretty sure it couldn't compare.

I rushed out the door like a teenager ready to attend a high school football game. I reached the last step and jumped down like Wonder Woman with my three-inch heels bouncing off the pavement.

I ran up to the car, screaming, "What's up, ladies?"

Michelle smiled at my enthusiastic response. "I see someone is happy about this trip."

"You better know it! I need this trip like a mouse needs cheese."

We threw our heads back and laughed as we sped down the highway heading toward Raleigh-Durham airport.

Natalia looked through the rearview mirror and asked, "So, did you pack those shorts that we talked about, young lady?"

I blushed at the thought of wearing such attire. "Yes, they're in the bag, but I can't say I will put them on."

Michelle turned around in her seat. "No one will care what you have on. Just relax and be free. This will be the first time since I've known you that you will not have to worry about church folk."

Natalia sighed. "I really wish you would understand that there is more to life than just church. God didn't make all this earth and splendor just to sit inside four walls and follow a bunch of nonsensical rules. God is real but some church folks ain't."

I didn't like where the conversation was going. "Church is all I know. It's in my blood. You need to try Jesus sometime yourself and stop with all the negative comments about church folk."

"We won't hold it against you, just loosen up and enjoy yourself," Natalia said with a smirk while looking through her rearview mirror.

We entered the parking area and found a space under the daily parking deck as the wooden barricade lifted to let us in. I stepped out of the car with a strut, feeling like America's next top model ready for a photo shoot. I put on my sunglasses as we grabbed our luggage and headed into the airport. We walked swiftly to the Delta kiosk to obtain our boarding passes. Since Natalia worked for the airlines, we had a greater advantage of getting through security quickly.

A TSA officer stepped up and said, "Greetings, ladies. Any computers or electronics in your bags?"

"No."

"Any bottles with more than three ounces of fluid?"
"No."

"All right then, please step into the body scanner."

Natalia didn't have to go through all the safety steps like we did. However, Michelle and I had to go through all the security requirements to foreign countries since this was our first time traveling outside of the United States.

I stepped in, throwing my hands up in the air. The scanner circled around my body and a green light appeared.

"You may step out, ma'am."

I looked around to see if everyone else had to do the same routine. I turned to Natalia and said, "I feel violated with all of this patting my body, removing my shoes and lifting my hands up."

"You really need to get some traveling experience under your belt. If you had TSA Pre-Check, this wouldn't be an issue. You're so behind the times."

We gathered all our carry-on items and headed toward the gate. I tried to keep up as my shoes slipped off my feet every step I made. I was thankful that I brought two pairs of sandals to change into. I stopped for a moment as the girls kept walking.

"Wait! I really need to change my shoes."

Michelle looked back. "I forgot to tell you not to wear your famous high heels. I bet your toes are on fire."

"How long is this flight?" I asked.

Natalia rolled her eyes as if she seemed irritated with my questioning. "It's about five hours give or take." She walked with speed as the backpack bounced around.

In spite of the great escape, my thoughts stayed on my long journey with Tommy and I wondered if sticking around all these years was worth the wait. I didn't like change and became very accustomed to our daily routine.

However, since having lots of time alone, I began to think more rationally. *Do I really allow him to walk over me? Have I really settled for someone who sleeps with other women? Could it be that he has a wife?*

We boarded the plane and found our seats. I viewed my ticket. "Seat thirteen F."

THAT CHURCH LIFE

Natalia threw her traveling bag in the top storage and said, "Lucky you, you get the window."

It dawned on me once I opened my window cover and sat down that maybe it was time to move on from Tommy. I didn't want to be like Ms. Olivia aka my biological mother. I wanted a happily-ever-after ending. All of the hurt, anxiety attacks, bruises, and disrespect came rushing into my thought process for some reason. I guess this was the first time in a long time that I could actually sit and think about it without distractions.

At that moment, I was honest with myself and didn't know if I could continue with Tommy Lee Davis.

It was 1:30 p.m. and we arrived at Montego Bay airport on time. Natalia was listening to her iPod and Michelle had fallen asleep. I was wide awake making decisions in my head about my life. I just needed to cut him off. That was all there was to it. But then reality hit. I knew that once I took one look at Tommy on an early Sunday morning playing that organ, I would be right back to square one: crazy in love.

I gazed out the window as we landed asking God to forgive me for my five-year brain freeze of stupidity and prayed that he would give me the strength to not suffer from that any longer.

"Whew, we made it, ladies! Jamaica, here we come!" Natalia screamed as she snatched her headphones off her ears.

I was enamored by the big palm trees. They swayed from side to side a few feet behind the airport wall.

I took my cell phone off airplane mode and noticed that I had six messages waiting. Curious to know who would be calling back to back, I listened to the voicemails.

"Hello? Hello?" The person calling hung up.

I listened to the next message.

"Missy, it's me, pick up, hun."

Finally, I recognized the faint voice after listening four consecutive times. It was Tommy whispering, sounding as if he had trouble gasping for air. He didn't sound very much like himself and was probably still weak from his surgery and all the injuries.

I blew out air as my lips bulged. Surprised, I tried desperately to erase his voice out of my head. I knew if I called back, I would be swooped into his witchcraft. I was determined to have fun on this trip and clear my mind from all my North Carolina troubles.

"So, where are we staying once we get off the plane?" I was now anxious to wear my two-piece bathing suit and walk into the beaming Jamaican sun.

Natalia reached into her bag and passed me a brochure. "We're going to a parish called Ocho Rios. It's where all the magic happens in Jamaica. Yeah mon!" She pumped her fist in the air as if she was part of the Black Panther party and proceeded to walk toward the immigration line.

"Passport, please."

We pulled out our passports and watched the immigration representative stamp our blue books. I had obtained my passport years ago waiting for a time such as this.

"Welcome to Jamaica, enjoy your trip."

Natalia responded back with a loud squeal, "Yeah mon! Follow me, ladies, you are about to have the time of your lives!"

We walked out of the airport and into the marvelous Jamaican light. We danced, reeled around in circles and jumped around as we glided down the walkway, ready to take part in this long-awaited spiritual uplift.

Chapter 13

We were expected to arrive at the plush, all-inclusive resort within two hours of our landing. A twelve-seater, white van pulled up in front of the airport and drove us, along with other travelers, to the resort's front door. The driver gave a thorough explanation of Jamaican landmarks and history as we passed by unfinished houses and mansions. He had a thick accent and talked very fast.

"What is he saying?"

"Missy, just pay attention. After listening to him for about twenty minutes, you will understand him well," Natalia said.

"Due to high interest on real estate loans, several families on the island decided to build their own homes by hand, brick by brick," he said. I was intrigued by the vast difference in culture. I took pictures while staying attentive to the stories of noticing the unidentifiable lines of rich and poor throughout each parish. One house might be a mansion-styled home and then two doors down we would see a house with a cloth covering roof with missing windows. The colorful bricks that were laid varied from house to house. Some houses had gates, while others had a large amount of rubble sitting in the front yards. Michelle looked through her window and said, "I think I could live here and enjoy the rest of my life."

"I don't know about that. I need to be near a mall and Walmart," Natalia said.

Michelle didn't seem surprised by Natalia's shallow response. "Well, when you grow up poor like I did, you can relate to living in situations like these."

"Yeah, I don't know anything about that," Natalia responded. Her daddy was a well-known attorney and her mother was a school administrator. She couldn't identify with Michelle's family's blue-collar lifestyles. I was disappointed with Natalia's lack of compassion for Michelle's past. "You can be truly self-centered sometimes. Anything will fly out of your mouth!"

"Is this coming from the girl who can't live without her compact? My mouth, that you now complain about, saved your narrow behind plenty of days in high school." Her hands flailed through the air. "If it wasn't for me, those little jealous girls would have pounced on your head and pulled all that long stringy hair every day after school."

"So, do I owe you something for your service?"

"Nope, not really; just respect my way of thinking and continue putting up with me. That's all for now," she replied as she looked directly at me while rolling her neck.

"You really need to be soaked in some holy oil."

"Oh, here we go."

"Here we go, what?" I looked over with a stern look, trying to figure out what the problem was.

"I need you to leave self-righteous Missy in North Carolina. I don't want to hear about oil, rebuking, or repentance this entire trip, you hear me? I need the hot and sexy Missy to come out for Jamaica!" Natalia said.

Michelle chuckled. "You should be glad someone cares about your soul, honey. At the rate you're going, there's no telling where you might end up."

Natalia turned to the side. "Well, look at the pot calling the kettle black. I don't recall you being holy and pure either, girlfriend."

Michelle slowly swung her head and looked at Natalia. "Let's not mess this gathering up with your foolish conversation. Understood?" The look Michelle gave meant don't start none, won't be none. She was subtle with her comebacks, but if you got her mad she didn't have a problem with putting you in your place. After being bullied as a young girl, she'd built confidence in middle school and learned how to handle people like Natalia. She became well respected and no one crossed the line once she gave the look.

"All right, ladies, you are now in the Ocho Rios parish. Your hotel is two miles ahead to your left." The driver cranked up the radio, now feeling comfortable to play his Jamaican rap music.

I rocked back and forth enjoying the unfamiliar beat.

THAT CHURCH LIFE

"Now this is music," Natalia said as she snapped her fingers. "What's your name, driver?" she asked.

"Beanie."

I was not expecting such a name for a muscle-built, tall, chocolate drop of a man. "Beanie? You from Jamaica?"

"Yes, most of my life here. But I spent a few of my early years in Queens, New York. I've been back and forth but I moved here permanently to help out when my mother became ill."

Not knowing the set-up for our Jamaican transportation, I said, "How sweet. Will you be our driver the whole time we're here, Beanie?"

"Only if you want me to, me lady."

"Me lady?" I sat looking confused.

"Yes, we say that out of respect when we talk to females."

I blushed as he started checking me out through the rearview mirror. "What's your name, me lady?"

Natalia nudged me in my side trying to get me to answer quicker.

"Missy."

"All right, Missy, my darling. We have made it to your destination. Here is my card, call me when you're ready to tour the Parish."

"Why thank you, Mr. Beanie."

Natalia whispered in my ear, "He's cute!"

"Yes, scrumptious even," I whispered back.

I took his card as we began to unload our items from the van.

"Let me help you, me lady." His smile was perfect along with his squeaky-clean white teeth. "Don't forget to call me, Ms. Beautiful Missy."

"I won't. I look forward to seeing you again."

"Did she really just say that out loud?" Michelle asked Natalia.

"Hey, what goes on in Jamaica stays in Jamaica. She will be calling you real soon, B!" Natalia blurted out with her hands on her hips.

We walked to the hotel's front door as our luggage rolled past us on a large cart. The hotel clerk placed everything in the lobby. He held his hand out as we identified our bags.

"Why is he doing that?" I asked.

Natalia walked past him and put ten dollars in his hand. "He's waiting for us to tip him. He won't leave until he gets his loot."

"What if you don't give it to him?"

"This is how he makes his living. He deserves every penny," she said.

Natalia paused and looked me up and down. "Girl, look at you! Get you from the church house for one day and you become an instant diva. Stick with me and I can raise you up from the church house to the penthouse, just like that."

"If I must keep self-righteousness in North Carolina, then you have to keep your hustling ways there also. Not in the mood for your *gangsta* boo attitude."

Changing the subject Natalia said, "Anyway! You put your church magic on Beanie, huh?"

Michelle stopped to say, "See, you just ignorant. Church and magic shouldn't even be in the same sentence."

I said, "I wouldn't say all that. No magic my way. I just found him to be very attractive, that's all."

Michelle gleamed. "Well, you always liked chocolate men. I don't know how you got involved with light-bright Tommy."

"Who?" I giggled. "It's a new day as they say on the Weight Watchers commercial. We never know what God has in store for us."

"Okay, preacher lady. I like how you're talking. I hope Tommy's yellow behind will be erased from your memory by the end of this trip," Natalia said as she walked with her fist balled up.

"You never know, my friend. I don't think Mr. Beanie is going to have people threatening to shoot him right before I preach. What was I thinking?"

The girls responded in unison, "You wasn't!"

"Let's go change clothes and head for the beach. Enough about me and my troubles. I'm leaving it all in the Lord's hands. Now, let's have some fun!"

Chapter 14

I was determined to make the best of the trip and release some strongholds that had taken over my life for so many years. Settling for Mr. Wrong out of convenience and keeping secrets was no longer an option for me. I wanted to remain saved, free and famous. My life had turned into a soap opera and it was time to wake up and smell the blue mountain coffee.

Being stuck on stupid in heels was not something that I wanted to talk about to the girls while vacationing, but I needed to talk about it from time to time to release some doubt and guilt from my system.

Spending quality time with my best friends in an exotic surrounding was the perfect scenario for some good girl chatter. We had a restful night's sleep during our first night in Jamaica and woke up to the sound of classical music playing in the hotel's hallway.

"With the music blasting out there, I guess that's our cue to get up and do something." Michelle fluffed her pillow and laid back down.

"I feel like I'm in Neiman Marcus with the soothing department store music ringing in my ears!" I growled, pulling the covers close to my chest.

Natalia jumped out of bed and walked around the room full of energy. She was wide open, as if she had a five-hour energy drink and looked ready to party. "All right, ladies! Chop, chop we have people to see and places to go. Wash your butts and let's head for the hills. There is too much to do here!" The room was filled with bright neon colors with palm tree wall paper. The double sinks with gold handles were made of marble that matched the floors. The ocean view patios would make even the non-swimmer take a chance and float on their back in the blue water for hours.

Michelle wiped her eyes as she yawned. "I'm hoping you don't have our entire day planned already, do you?"

Natalia pulled out a notebook filled with activities. "Don't act like we just met yesterday! I'm always prepared. I didn't plan for Missy to meet her man so I will need to pencil in some time for her new boo."

I looked up with a wrinkled face. "Geesh, I just met the guy and now he is my man?"

Natalia threw her hands up as if she had a magical wand. "Speak it into the air and it shall come to pass." She laughed at her own joke while picking her teeth with floss.

Michelle got out of bed and moved around slowly, looking exhausted with sweat beads all over her face. She turned to me with raised eyebrows. "I hope you call him, Missy. We can't have you going back home chanting Tommy's name, that's for sure. We tend to forget that God has bigger and better for us, but we ourselves get in the way of our own blessings."

"Preach, chile, preach!" Natalia shouted as she stomped her foot and waved her hand imitating Mother Gaines.

We all laughed at the visual, then shuffled around the room trying to get ourselves together.

"I hear you loud and clear, my friend. I'm almost positive that I have interfered with several of my blessings. I just always feel obligated to help people become better and I forget about what I need to do for myself. That's just the minister in me, I guess."

"Well, you can't keep helping others when you're not altogether. Sometimes you have to help yourself, too." Michelle patted me on the back as if she was clearing my lungs.

"I guess you're right. You live and you learn. Tommy left four messages last night. What should I do?"

Natalia's eyes widened. "Is that a trick question? I'm trying to get deliverance from cursing so much so please don't ask me questions like that."

"Michelle, do you have an answer since you are more sensible?" Natalia rolled her eyes as she stuck her tongue out at Michelle.

Michelle stood up near the bedroom mirror while flat-ironing her hair. She paused and said, "If I had a man who was good for nothing, I wouldn't respond. Move on. End of story!" She seemed as if the conversation vexed her soul as she slammed the curlers down onto the vanity.

I dropped my head as a pain shot up to my heart. It was as if a dagger poked me right in the center of my chest and ripped down to my stomach. It was true; it was time to unlock the controlling spirits that locked me into this relationship. I flashed back to the red flags that started to appear early on in our relationship.

Five years ago...

"Do you love me, Tommy?"

"Of course, I do. We have been together for six months and you're still questioning how I feel about you, girl? I could be with anyone on this campus, but I chose you."

"Well, I was just wondering. My sorority sisters tell me all the time that you flirt with everyone on campus."

"Missy, don't be stupid. Women who don't have a man are always trying to mess it up for the women who do. Get that mess out of your head. It's me and you, kid, forever."

"All right, enough about all that," I said, snapping back to the present. "I have other things to share with the two of you. I didn't want to pour on too much before the fun began."

"What? You pregnant?" Natalia asked.

"Heck no. I made one mistake being crazy in love with the wrong one. I'm not about to make a second mistake and get knocked up without being married!"

"Honey, even if you were married, I wouldn't advise having babies by that unstable creature," Natalia said with sarcasm.

Michelle came to my defense. "I have faith in you that you wouldn't do anything that crazy. Chill out, Natalia. No need to reiterate the same thing over and over again to her like she's your child. I'm sure she gets it now." Michelle shook her head as she sucked her teeth.

"Well, I want to make sure that she isn't going back to him when we get home, that's all. She lied to me months ago telling me that they were finished. I was hurt to find out that the manic relationship continued, knowing that man is sleeping with all of Durham."

"You act like you ain't never stayed with someone who wasn't good for you. What about Dwayne?" I leaned back, waiting for a response.

Natalia's eyes shifted to the other side of the room as she licked her lips. "Let's not go there, okay. My situation was different. Dwayne decided he liked men but at least he didn't beat me."

Feeling irritated, I added, "Must I say this one more time! He didn't beat me. He was acting in self-defense! Ugh!" I grunted as I punched the pillows on my bed.

THAT CHURCH LIFE

I was always fighting with him. Every now and again I would throw the first punch and would try my best to scratch out an eye for cheating on me. I hoped that he would never look at another woman again. Or sometimes I would go as far as pulling out patches of his hair so that he wouldn't be so attractive. He didn't hesitate to fight back. Thus, leaving me all bruised up for the world to see.

Natalia kept talking as my flashbacks continued. "Yeah, but a black eye, though? You weigh all of one hundred and twenty pounds. No big old curly-headed man needs to be giving you black eyes, much less using self-defense methods."

"All right, enough. Let's just get dressed and get out of here. You two are playing tit for tat. Get it together so we can go out and enjoy the sun," Michelle said.

Several minutes later, we were fully dressed in our beach gear and ready to eat breakfast. The hotel had a restaurant that served food all day long. We grabbed an assortment of food from fruits and grains to oatmeal porridge, then we found a cozy table that sat directly in front of the beach. After we slid into our seats, we sat in silence, assessing the blue waves rising high beside us.

I stuck a piece of cantaloupe in my mouth and said, "I think I will call Beanie to come and join me for lunch." Natalia put her spoon down on the table and looked up.

"I have planned the entire day for us up until sundown. You might want to let him know that he can come and see you around 8:00 p.m. That's our only opening."

"Opening? And when did you become my mother?" I pulled my phone out of my purse.

"Hello."

"Hello, may I speak to Beanie?"

"Hello, me lady!"

"You know who this is?"

"Why of course. The one and only beautiful Missy from the Carolina's. How are you, my dear?"

I grinned. "I'm doing great now that I've heard your voice." I winked at Michelle as she tuned into our conversation. Natalia was more concerned about adding six packets of sugar to her blue mountain coffee as she twirled her curly fro.

"I would like to see you today, me lady. Would it be possible to stop by after I get off work?" His voice was deeper over the phone than in person.

Twirling my oatmeal, I said, "Yes, that would be perfect. What time?"

"Around nine."

"Great!"

"All right, see you soon, beautiful."

Clearing my throat, I said, "See you soon, handsome." I heard a beep alerting me that I had another call waiting on the other line. I clicked over as Natalia burped loudly before gulping down her coffee.

"Hello?"

"Hi there, sweetie."

My heart sank and my smile quickly left my lips. It was Tommy, interrupting my positive vibe once again just like the devil's imp.

"Hi, Tommy. How are you?"

"I would be better if you were here. My brother told me that you tried to visit a few days ago. What happened, did you give up on me? You never came back."

"No. I didn't. When I called to check on you the second time, your brother said it wasn't a good time to come up yet."

Natalia motioned to hang up the phone as she hissed at me.

"You sound good," I said with hesitation. Better than I thought he would sound.

"Yes, it's been a journey to recover from all of this." He moaned in agony. "Are you coming by to see me today?"

"Umm, actually I'm on vacation with the girls right now."

"Vacation?"

"Yes, Natalia surprised us with an all-expense paid trip to Jamaica!"

"Oh, is that so?" He paused, "So I guess you couldn't postpone that until I healed, huh?"

I stomped my foot, irritated. "Well, I figured it was a good time to clear my head considering all that happened that night."

"I see."

"Well, I don't mean to cut you off, honey, but this is an international call. I will chat with you when I return, okay?"

I could tell he was clenching his teeth. "Yeah, whatever."

"Bye!"

When I hung up, Natalia said, "I'm sure he is feeling so neglected. Poor cray cray," she chuckled, looking over at me with a devilish grin.

"Yeah, he didn't sound too happy." I spooned some oatmeal into my mouth. As I rolled my eyes, I added, "Oh well, not my problem. What's next?"

The girls looked at each other then back at me. I was not going to show any emotion around them. I had to put on my big girl panties and carry on.

"Proud of you, sis," Michelle said with watery eyes.

"Ditto!" Natalia expressed with sincere happiness.

We got up from the table and raced each other to the beach with full bellies. Flip-flops and bathing suits were seen all over the beach. The sand rubbed across my feet as the wind pushed me forward.

Natalia shook her finger as she swished sand everywhere and said, "It needs to be an unspoken understanding that Tommy Lee Davis will no longer be a part of our conversation during this trip."

"We hear you, Boss Lady. No need to keep laying down ground rules," Michelle said as she kicked sand fiercely onto Natalia's feet. I plopped my body into the sand in the middle of the walkway path made by other tourists. I was ready to make sand art as we came closer and closer to the water. Big white birds flew high above us as the sky remained clear and blue.

I could no longer hold my secret inside. The phone call from Tommy stirred up so many emotions all at once. I looked up at the clouds wondering how a mother could not make a better attempt to be with her daughter. A man and a verbal agreement wouldn't keep me from my child. I now wanted to talk about my mother to the others. It was time since emotionally, I was all over the place. I blurted out, "Sylvia Jones was not my real mother."

"What the… Now that was random," Natalia said, shifting the sand through her hands.

Michelle stopped kicking the sand over her ankles and looked over. "Say what? Repeat that again?"

I began to sulk into my sorrow while finishing the first layer of my sand castle. "My biological mother showed up at the church on Sunday and told me everything. From the time she met my father, all the way until when she had to give me up. I didn't believe her at first, so I went to Mother Smithfield. Yeah, it's true, she isn't my biological mother. Sylvia is actually my cousin, not my mother."

Natalia shook her head back and forth. "Dang, that's pretty sad. But I told you Mother Smithfield had the juice. She knows everything. A true gossiping goddess." She lifted her hands toward the sky.

"Natalia, hush! This is not the time for your sarcastic humor," Michelle said. She threw the sand down and reached for me. "Are you okay, though, Missy?"

"Yeah, I will make it. Keeping it to myself was the exhausting part. I'm going to eventually talk to my dad about it. I just don't know when."

"This doesn't seem logical at all. Why would Pastor Jones keep important information like this to himself? And why haven't you talked to him yet instead of going to the gossiping bird first?" Michelle asked.

"I am just not ready to talk to him yet. I am sure he kept it to himself because he knew she would have ruined his name. You know how he feels about that. All I know is if I didn't know Jesus, I would be at Butner Hospital in a special white jacket right about now."

Natalia blew her breath. "Well thank God for Jesus 'cause ain't no way my pops would be able to get away with something like that. I would have found out right after birth. My family can't hold nothing."

"Ha! And neither can you. It's all in your bloodline," I said.

I unwrapped my towel from my waist and stretched it out as my back hit the ground. I flapped my arms up and down like a bird creating a sand angel. When I stopped, I said, "I know my daddy is a good man. I'm sure he did all of this to protect me."

"Protect you? Or protect the church?" Natalia asked as she picked up her cell phone to take pictures of the tiny yellow fish that were swimming nearby.

"Either way, it's water under the bridge now. I loved Sylvia and she will always be my mother no matter what my birth certificate says. She loved me, this I know."

Michelle leaned back. "Yes, she sure did, sis. She spoiled you rotten. Let these crazy and challenging experiences make you a better woman and preacher. God has a plan and obviously he will be granting a greater life for you than your father ever had. I believe this is only a test to get you to the next level of your anointing."

"Didn't I say not to mention church stuff on this trip? I don't want to hear about being anointed, appointed, or exploited." Natalia shrugged.

I swung my neck around. "Exploited? Did you just add that in because it rhymed?"

"Yep."

"That Durham High School teaching truly failed you, sis. You just wait until we get back home to the Bull City. I am going to put you on that altar as soon as the church doors swing open."

"You're really messing up the ambiance right now." She turned away. "I need a drink. Hell, where is Bob Marley when you need him?"

"You definitely don't need anything or anyone affiliated with Bob Marley. I've seen you in that state before. Not a good look for you, honey. You need Jesus," I said.

Michelle nodded in agreement.

We sat back and laughed as the sun beamed brightly over the pretty Carolina-blue sea. We talked for hours as Natalia sipped on every drink given to her by the roving bartender. There were waiters and waitresses walking in the sand, offering food, drink and towels every ten minutes. We felt like royalty while listening to the islanders in the background. We didn't have to move if we didn't want to. It felt good.

"I wish that life could be like this every day," Michelle sighed.

I pushed my sunglasses to the tip of my nose and looked over them, "Love, friends, laughter and God. A perfect combination."

Natalia, with glossy eyes from all the drinking, said, "Don't forget to add a joint or two onto that happy list you got going on."

The laughter was continuous, and we enjoyed every minute of it. I loved my friends. They were my sisters until the end.

THAT CHURCH LIFE

Chapter 15

The sun set, a quarter moon arose and shined brightly. The reflection of the hotel rested on the calm ocean. I walked outside and sat at a picnic table waiting for Beanie to arrive. I felt a little uncomfortable meeting a complete stranger alone while wearing my two-piece bathing suit. But at this point, what did I have to lose? The girls decided to attend the dolphin show without me.

Soon after I rubbed Vaseline on my lips, he walked onto the hotel patio. Beanie Anderson appeared smack dab in front of my lusting eyes wearing a New York Giants tank top, Tommy Hilfiger shorts, a pair of black Jordan's and a baseball cap with the letter "B" written in bright green lettering. His urban ensemble was a turn-on as I watched him walk with a slight dip in his step.

He sat beside me and I inhaled his cologne. "Greetings, me lady. Don't you look beautiful?"

My chest stood at attention as my bathing suit gripped my breasts from the new fullness. My boobs stood straight up as if I had them lifted like Toni Braxton. I covered my flesh with a sheer over shirt but it still allowed a clear visual of my belly and upper thighs. Not the kind of bathing suit you wear on a church beach trip. His eyes traveled as he tried to play it off by looking quickly back up to my face. He hugged me tightly and I embraced his strong chest, melting like a stick of butter when his arms wrapped completely around me. I knew this wasn't very "ministerial-like" but my human flesh gave in to the dark chocolate man candy that rubbed up close to me. Sexual thoughts began to formulate, and I attempted to replace them with a bible verse.

"So good to see you again, sweetness. How was your day?"

"Oh, it just got better now that I am here with you." I blushed, becoming self-conscious and putting my arms around my midsection to hide my Jet Magazine Beauty of the week visual.

"So, tell me about yourself, me lady?"

"I don't know where to begin. You already know I'm from North Carolina, born and raised. I'm a minister at my dad's church and I work as a project manager in my home town. What about you?"

"Not much to tell. I'm a hard worker who loves family. I changed my life around a few years ago after getting into trouble a lot in my youth. I gave my life to Christ and I'm also a leader at my church."

My eyes sparkled. "Oh really! So you can relate to that church life, huh? What are some of the things you changed about yourself?" First man I'd met in a long time who knew the Lord. He might be a keeper.

"Yeah mon, I became an evangelist last year. I drive all throughout the island helping the poor. It made my mom's heart glad. For real, mon. God has worked through me and moved all the mess in my life. Never married, no children that I know of, life is good, me lady. God is good," he said as he pointed up to the sky, acknowledging his redeemer. There were at least thirty other people walking on the beach, holding hands. It was truly a romantic scene to see all the love in the air. I drooled at his silky lips moving while he talked. He whispered sweet nothings in my ear with those lips as they gently touched the top of my ear lobe. They felt so soft and seemed kissable. He broke me out of my trance when he said, "You're just so beautiful. I know you have a boyfriend back home."

"Believe it or not, I don't. I just broke up with someone after being together five years." *Cross your fingers, girl. Now you know you lying with a straight face!* "So, do you ever go back to the States?"

"Why yes, at least once a month. I have siblings spread out all over."

"That's nice. I'm an only child. I bet having siblings is a good thing."

"Not always." He chuckled as he reached for my hand.

I looked down at his smooth hands as his gentle touch caught me off guard. I rubbed his hand back gently while thinking about having his babies. "Well, at least you have family that you can turn to."

We talked for hours about family, careers, his mistakes, my mistakes, relationships and future plans. He was a gentle soul and a very kind-hearted person. He didn't have a problem talking about the crimes he committed while being an immature young man. From gangbanging and robbery, to car theft, he did it all. He was so thankful to be a saved and a changed man. No kids, no other women, no problems, eerie!

We ended our date with a long heartfelt hug and kiss that sent me to the moon and back, like shooting summer fireworks. I just spent hours with a true knight in shining armor and I wanted this feeling to last forever. He promised to visit me each night while I was on vacation. I didn't know it then, but he would keep his word.

By day, I toured Dunn's River Falls and Mystic Mountain with the girls laughing and joking like children. By night I danced, cuddled and shared my deepest wants and dreams for my future with Mr. Beautiful. He understood my calling and the sacrifices I had to make for the church. He also understood my passion concerning elevation to pastoral duties and one day uplifting my father's legacy. We shared views on church vices and stereotypes that seemed world renowned. For the first time, I could talk to someone who understood my spiritual wants and needs.

He embraced me every night, giving me assurances that everything was going to be all right just like Bob Marley sang: "Don't worry 'bout a thing, cause every little thing is going to be all right."

Once I talked out my problems, I felt motivated and revived. After this encounter, my life would not be the same.

On this day, with only a few hours left before departing from this paradise, I wanted to remain in his arms forever, but reality hit. I had to get back to Durham to finish preparing for the next church engagement. It was time for the Fifth Sunday Jubilee.

Chapter 16

We arrived back in the United States late Saturday evening. I was overjoyed thinking about the upcoming Sunday service and ready to receive a blessing. My new acquaintance remained heavy on my mind and I couldn't wait to call him once I arrived home. I entered my apartment building, picked up my cat and fed him as he purred.

"No place like home, right, Twinkles?"

I was ready to make the call, desperately longing to hear his voice. He answered and his "hello" gave me chills. For several hours, we contemplated how to make our long-distance friendship work. After a few hours, I looked up at the clock on my dresser and reality to set back in. It was 3:00 in the morning. I was mesmerized and wanted to hear more, but I knew I had to cut the conversation short for some proper beauty sleep. My goal was to attend Sunday school, but it didn't seem very feasible at this point. I told him goodbye, then, set my alarm, rolling over.

Alone again.

I had to shake this love bug and get back to a minister's mindset.

THAT CHURCH LIFE

The alarm sounded off like a wailing fire truck siren at exactly 9:00 a.m. I jumped up frightened and fumbled around zombie style. I tried to get ready for the big day at church as fast as I could.

Every Fifth Sunday, the local churches came together displaying church spirit in psalm, dance and mime. The Mt. Zion Holiness church members were pumped for this event and ready to give God a high praise. The older saints gathered up family members as they rushed through the front wooden doors to experience such a spectacular event.

I entered the church at 9:55, after driving eighty-five miles per hour to ensure a timely entrance. Feeling sluggish, I pushed myself to be cordial while giving members my parade hand wave and cheek-to-cheek smile. I glimpsed at the first row and squared my shoulders trying to shake off the sleep monster.

I ran over to Mother Gaines, shouting, "I am ready to do some churchin'! How about you, Mother?"

Mother waved her handkerchief high in the air, confirming that she was ready, too.

"Well, don't you look beautiful? This is going to be a fine time with the Lord, gal. You just wait and see. Shundo!"

"I believe it and receive it. I'm ready to get the Holy Ghost party started."

"You singing today, gal?" She sucked on her peppermint with a wide grin.

"No, ma'am. I think the choir will take over today."

She slumped back in her seat, disappointed at my response. "All right, I will request a song or two next time. How does that sound, sweetness?"

I leaned over and said, "Yes, ma'am. I will be ready."

I walked with dignity and pride in my new purple silk outfit that flowed beyond my ankles as I greeted everyone. My hair was pressed straight and slicked down nicely. One would think that I had a Dark N Lovely relaxer slapped in my head the night before. Glitter sparkled on my purple stiletto heels as I tried to keep my balance giving hugs to familiar faces. I was tempted to click them three times just to see if I would land in Kansas. Cute little Dorothy had nothing on me. My eyelids drooped, I felt lethargic, but I seemed to always work the crowd no matter what. My twenty-seven-year-old body felt limp, giving the signal that sleep deprivation was coming down the mountain. I knew napping in the study wouldn't be possible. I walked slowly, scanning the entire church. The decorations I helped to create weeks ago were still placed around the exterior, resembling the Harvard Museum of Natural History. Every empty space displayed purple flowers, purple candles and purple bows to fulfill the state-of-the-art look of our church gallery. The arrangements resembled a twentieth-century theatre wedding with a touch of elegance.

"You worked hard on these decorations," Michelle said, standing behind me.

THAT CHURCH LIFE

"Hey, sis, I didn't see you walk in," I replied as I fluffed a batch of flowers sitting on the back table of the sanctuary.

"I know all of this purple was your idea since it's your favorite color."

I wiped dust from a top shelf display and said, "The decorating committee worked hard on this grandiose scenery. I can't take all the credit. But I made sure before I left the country that everything was in tip-top shape."

While we continued to chat, several visitors arrived early to take pictures with family members in front of the famous awe-inspiring flower collection. Michelle followed me around as we watched individuals rush from picture snapping to scrambling in search of the perfect seat. They waited patiently to hear a word from the Lord as they talked amongst each other, keeping their volume below a whisper. Head officials walked in together, bowing their heads saying, "God bless you," to everyone in passing.

I had asked Michelle to be in attendance to back up the musicians, if needed. She looked beautiful as her rosy brown cheeks were colored with a tinge of rouge. Her hair, full of pin curls, along with her shiny purple lip gloss, added to her look. She wore a sheer purple blouse with a black skirt that touched her knees. She wasn't a fan of heels as she wore her Mary Jane's with black tights.

We stood in the back waiting for Natalia. She also agreed to join us since she had the weekend off. Natalia entered a few minutes later with a long flowing, B33 wig and a purple headband around her forehead. She didn't like wearing make-up, but her face was always crystal clear of acne and blemishes. She pranced next to us, wearing a black short-sleeved silk shirt and a purple mini skirt with high open-toed black heels.

"It must be sista day!" Michelle shouted, looking Natalia up and down.

Trying to keep my eyes open, I said in a slow voice, "Well, look a here! Greetings, my beautiful sistas!"

"Don't you look nice and tired? Long night? I can tell by all this pageantry that we are going to be here for a long time, huh?" Natalia asked in disgust.

She didn't enjoy church hoopla and was always in a hurry to get church over with each time she paid a visit.

Michelle became teary-eyed. "It feels strange to be here together after all these years. I miss being in church with you guys. I kinda miss this place."

"Yeah, as children it seemed like we were here every time the doors were unlocked. Heaven bound!"

Natalia quickly said, "I realized right after high school that it doesn't take all of this to get to heaven. Thank God for flight attendant school rescuing me from church slavery."

"Church slavery? Okay, smarty pants. Did you ever figure out what it will take to get to heaven since being in church won't help?" I asked with my arms folded.

"Minister Girlfriend, I have learned more than you can ever imagine since I left this place. Worship Network got me covered."

"Uh huh," Michelle said as she rubbed her eyes. "I'm glad to see all of us together again, now I feel charged to give God some serious praise!"

I lifted my leg up in the air and swung my head back.

Michelle laughed as her skirt moved up and down. "You look so pumped up, girl. I'm sure you have a word of hope and encouragement at the tip of your tongue, don't you?"

"Yep!" I pretended I had a microphone close to my mouth. "God's producing miracles today and we won't leave here the same way we came. Glory!"

Michelle clapped as if she were watching a dramatic screenplay. "Amen, sister, preach!"

Natalia sighed, not finding anything we said amusing. "You're such an old spirit in a young woman's body. Seriously?"

I chuckled as we all headed toward the far-left side of the church to find a seat for the girls.

"I guess it isn't a question of where you will sit; right in the pulpit with your daddy as always," Natalia said.

"My designated space in the place! Don't be a hater all your life, sis." I walked straight to the pulpit with my eyes on the big honorary chairs and bright pulpit lighting. I stepped up to the platform as my daddy leaned over to help me. "Hello, sweet daughter."

I tilted my hand as he grabbed it, straining to walk up the steps. "Hello, Daddy."

He handled me with care so that I wouldn't trip up the stairs. "The church looks beautiful," he mumbled.

I looked over at him in disgust, biting my tongue. I couldn't wait to address the family secret. "Yes, it does, the purple roses add a nice touch to the décor."

"Lord knows you probably had to order all of these purple roses from another country. Where do they sell an abundance of purple roses in Durham?" he asked.

Not really interested in his small talk, I winked, not trying to show emotion or reveal my décor secrets of getting help from the older missionaries to complete the job. "You would be surprised, Daddy."

We sat and watched each row fill up with colorful outfits and hats. The older ladies paid close attention to the clock above the pulpit to ensure that we started on time. They looked at the clock, then back at Daddy again, giving him the subtle signal to start the service. All local ministers piled into the pulpit two minutes before the clock struck 11:00 am.

THAT CHURCH LIFE

The musicians turned their eyes to the pulpit, hoping to get a head nod to start the entrance music. The ushers were busy as they walked up and down the front aisle, ordering people to sit in the remaining empty seats. Fans were passed out along with an envelope for special gifts, tithes and offerings. The officials lined up at the front door for their Fifth Sunday Jubilee march.

Mother Smithfield sat moving her head up and down as she watched everyone coming and going. She loved Fifth Sunday Jubilee and always became emotional. Nothing but death could ever take her from it. All her friends were dead and gone; they used to love coming together for the grand event.

She gritted her teeth, trying to get Daddy's attention. She wanted him to hurry up and give the orders to start the service. She stared at him, clearing her throat. Finally, from her seat she blurted out, "It's time, Passa."

He nodded his head, acknowledging her blatant request.

Meanwhile, the musicians started playing as if they were part of the NC Jazz Festival. Michelle's eyes were glazed as she watched their every move. She played the organ years ago for Mt. Zion and was considered Tommy's back up. But right after leaving high school, she never played for us again. We figured she just outgrew us and wanted to move on. She was better than Tommy and could get down on the keys playing everything in "C". She kept glancing over at the musicians as if she wanted to slide across the organ and start playing. I knew before the service was over, she was going to inch over to the keys and rock the house.

At 11:05 a.m., the officials lined up and the rest was history. The lines were color coordinated by title. The ministers wore black and white and walked in first. The deacons wore black and gold, looking fierce with gold shimmery ties tucked inside their black tuxedo suits. The female elders wore all white suits with white matching hats, looking pure and divine. The male elders wore all white suits with white shiny shoes and black heel taps. The missionaries wore white and red as they trickled along slowly behind the male elders. Last, but not least, the pastors and bishops marched in solid gold and purple robes, kingdom royalty. All involved were dressed to impress, waving flags, whistles, tambourines and washboards, bouncing to the fast-marching band music.

The organ, drums, cymbals, bongos, washboard, tambourines and keyboard were all in one accord. The drum beat along with the "A" key base line on the organ, had the church bouncing. Elder Rhonda Snipes, the show stopper, dipped as she walked down the aisle. The middle-aged diva carried herself like a dignified Presbyterian and was admired by many. Although she had Christ in her life, she flaunted around the church trying to get her groove back. She wore extravagant and provocative outfits that enticed the deacons to "assist" her at all times. The eyes of the church officials widened as she continued to give a glide with every stride. Every outfit she wore matched her big oversized hat that she could barely keep balanced as it wobbled on the top of her head.

She was loud and boisterous each time she opened her mouth. She talked to herself as she strutted down the runway. "Oh glory. Help me, Lord! Hey. Hey. Hey. Do it, God!" Her boobs swished from side to side in sync with her highly sanctimonious animation. She screamed and stomped as her head sparkled with sweat and the nonstop head bobbing seemed to make everyone dizzy as they watched her closely. The pushpins stationed in her Tina Turner straight wig kept it all together nice and neat. With her thigh-hugging skirt that dropped right above her big hammock knees, she could barely move, but she played it off well, swishing from side to side with dignity.

The congregation egged her on because they found her animated performance very entertaining. "Work it, Elder."

"Look a here, look a here."

"Ah shucks, she has done it again."

Her designated seat was near the left wall, aligned with three rows of pews. These particular pews were turned horizontally from the rest of the church seating. Sister Angela, who was the church secretary, slipped Elder Rhonda a handkerchief to cover her big mama jama's after she got settled. The deacons sat directly across from Elder Snipes looking up the side of her skirt every chance they got. Deacon Freemon especially took a deep swallow as he scanned her row. He choked from discomfort, putting his head down as he wiped the saliva off his lips. He leaned over to the other deacons, discussing her sexiness as Daddy looked at me shaking his head. "Now she knows she is too old for all that prancing. She got these men in here acting like heathens!"

Deacon Freeman's eyebrows caved in, and he pushed his false teeth into place as he continued to stare. She looked up and winked at him as if to say, "Call me later, sugah."

Once the strutting contest ended, the musicians gave a hand signal holding up two fingers to change the speed of the music. The congregation rocked and jumped out of control as if it was a KISS rock concert.

Michelle walked up front, sliding onto the organ. She had to get a piece of this bounce music action. The musicians switched places immediately. They acknowledged her as the queen of the Hammond SK2. The choir clapped when she arrived for the challenge. They were pumped to sing with her. Michelle dropped a familiar beat as the choir sang loudly and the tambourines moved in full force.

"When I think of Jesus and all he's done for me...

When I think of Jesus and how he set me free...

I can dance, dance, dance, dance, dance, dance, dance, all night!"

Michelle held the "C" note down with her left fingers, tapping the base cords lightly. The drummer followed, and it was as if she had never left us. Her fingers floated across the keys with ease. The drummer was feeling it as he dropped his head down shaking his Rastafari dreads each time his stick touched the snare. The washboard and tambourine were in unison. They played with precision and power. The congregation hollered, jumped around, and yelled, losing all control.

My daddy couldn't stop smiling while tapping his feet to the music. It was imperative that he grabbed the microphone to say something during the praise session. He didn't just want to be seen, he also wanted to be heard.

"I know the program prepared is created for the purpose of bringing decency and order in this place, but good God, we all know it is subject to change due to the leading of the Holy Ghost. Good God Almighty!" he shouted and shook the microphone in the air. He skipped around the pulpit on one foot as if he was trying to find his balance. We didn't need two speakers for the hour as he looked tempted to say a word that would bring the house down. He screamed at the top of his lungs, holding his handkerchief in his left hand and wiped sweat off his forehead. "I feel the Holy Ghost moving deep down in my soul, Church. Lord have mercy, Lord. I said it's like fiyah shut up in my bones. Lord have mercy. Help us, Lord." As he continued to jiggle, he waved hands from side to side, shouting, and speaking in tongues. Natalia sat looking irritated. Her facial expressions revealed that she was ready to move on to the next part of the service. We made eye contact as she rolled her eyes and glared as if it was my fault that the Holy Ghost took over the church. Daddy passed the microphone to Minister Joseph who was the master of ceremony for the service. He spoke loudly, ignoring the praise session and moved on with the service. "Now it's time for the Church of America Combined Choir to sing another selection."

"Amen!"

He pulled out a dollar bill from his wallet and continued to babble, "After the choir sings, we can get ready for the part of service where everyone can participate and that is offering. Amen?" The congregation fumbled through their wallets and purses following his command. The choir stood up and sang Andréa Crouch's, "Oh Happy Day." Mother Mary Barclay led the song as the choir swayed back and forth to the music. She was one of the best singers in the church and her vocal chords were strong. She had a baritone that could put a lot of men to shame.

"Oooohhhhhh Happy Dayyyy."

"You betta sang, Mother!" Mother Gaines shouted.

The sound echoed throughout the church as Mother Barclay held the microphone away from her mouth. She belched out notes so hard you could see her throat tremble. Her voice was a cross between Donna Summer and Gladys Knight depending on the key that the song was played in. Her high notes put the church right back into square one of praise and worship.

When the song came to a close, Mother ended it with, "Oh Yeah," and aligned it to blend into the ending note.

"You got this, Mother, bring us on home," Minister Joseph shouted. "Now it's time for the most important part of the service. We've danced, sang and hollered, but now let's give God another form of praise for our offering."

The praise dance team used this time of the service to run around the entire 6,500-square foot church with their flags.

Pastor Jason Jenkins, the head pastor of the Holy Covenant Organization, was the speaker of the hour. He sat in the head chair waiting for the offering to end. He jumped up and grabbed the microphone to speak without any introduction.

He went into preaching mode immediately. "Turn to your neighbor and say, neighbor, this is some good church right here. My God, my God! Are yawl ready for the word?"

"Yes, bring it on, Pastor," Mother Gaines shouted as she balled up her fists with excitement and raised them in the air.

"Lift up your sword, known as your bibles to the Lord and let's begin to read." The Pastor gave the chapter and scripture. Then, he said, "Elder Rhonda, you ready to read?"

She slowly stood as she moved her tight skirt downward, screaming, "Yes, Passa, I'm ready," as she fluttered her thick eyelashes.

"I will be coming from the book of St. John chapter one, verse three. When you have it, say amen."

"Amen, amen, amen," rang throughout the congregation.

"If I had to choose a topic this morning, my topic would be…he made a way out of no way."

"Amen, you better work that word, Pastor!" Elder Snipes said.

"See, in spite of all the troubles around us, folks giving up on God, he made it so that we can always look to him to be our own light within our darkness."

"Hallelujah!" Mother Gaines shouted. She looked ready to roll on the floor.

"You talking good now, Preacha," Mother Taylor said.

With Godly confidence, he responded back, "I know I am. Watch me work this word, saints." The audience laughed. "See, God made a promise and we got to hold on to what he said. Can I get a witness?" He jumped down from the pulpit and hit the floor of the church, cocking his head back like a turkey buzzard.

He screamed, "Oh I can't get no help over here."

Every time a pastor used those words, the entire church stood to their feet with the intent to help out.

"Preach, Pastor, preach!" I shouted, all into the word. He walked down the aisle with a hard stomp that made the floor shake. His perspiration flung right on to the people in the sanctuary like little drops of rain that soon became a mini shower for the church mothers.

His adjutant ran to get him paper towels before it became a mini rainstorm on the front pew. When the pastor noticed his bodily fluids had traveled onto the ladies' clothing, he paused and said, "Excuse me, ladies, for the rain. I got to get this word out of my system. Hallelujah! Look at your neighbor and say, 'Neighbor, he made a way out of no way for you and for me. So you gotta hold on to his unchanging hand!'" He shook the microphone in his hand. "I say, is there one here today who's ready to give their life to such a good God? Don't let the devil have you!" he screamed. "God made it so. Hold on saints of God, hold on! Do I have someone who would like to keep holding on? Or do I have someone who wants to know him as a personal savior?"

He eyeballed the congregation as several individuals walked to the pulpit. He examined the ones coming his way and shouted, "See there, God is still in the soul-saving business and he is moving up in this place."

"Amen, Pastor!" the congregation shouted.

"Let's make the devil mad and sneak a dance in before everyone comes up to the altar!" he shouted, cocking his head back again.

The music started and Michelle was getting full enjoyment, hitting the "C" note for the quick two-minute praise. Everyone bowed their heads all at once and commenced to performing another holy dance.

Natalia stood up with her arms folded. Several members walked to the front of the church to give their lives to Christ. Other individuals came up for a refreshing word of prayer. Pastor's helper grabbed the holy oil and passed it to him for a traditional ceremony of oil wiping and swiping on each individual's forehead.

"All it takes is one touch of the Master's hand." His strong burly hands had some folks shuffling their feet searching for balance. Some held it together while others fell straight to the ground like flies. He was a strong, dark chocolatey man, about six-foot-four and easy on the eyes for the church ladies. He had a deep voice like Barry White that would carry throughout the congregation. Each time he performed laying-on of the hands, the spirit would move like a lightning bolt. Member after member went down for the count.

As he continued to minister, Elder Rhonda stood close by him puckering her lips at his chocolatey goodness. I could see her nasty thoughts inside her head. I knew what her facial expressions meant since I used to wear that same expression when thinking about a man. I walked to the altar and stood beside her as her lust bug became obvious to everyone in the pulpit.

She whispered, "He shole look scrumptious, Lawd have mercy on my soul."

I put my hand over my mouth trying not to giggle while in the presence of the Lord. "I know how you feel, honey, but folks are staring at you from the pulpit. Get yourself together."

THAT CHURCH LIFE

She snapped back immediately. She took her hands and moved her skirt down to cover her knees and positioned herself back into church girl formation. She looked up at me with thankful eyes.

The service came to a close after the final prayer. Pastor Jenkins and the head bishop stood at the front door of the congregation in preparation of shaking everyone's hands and invited individuals to the Jubilee dinner.

The dinner was cooked downstairs in the church dining hall area. The smell of collard greens, ham hocks, fried chicken and chitterlings floated right into the congregation. The church dining hall was ready to receive the congregation immediately after dismissal. Within five minutes of arrival, a variety of southern food was served.

"May we bow our heads in a word of prayer?" Bishop Jenkins suggested as he stood near the head dining room table with his hands up in the air in reverencing God. He started every prayer with, "Father God."

"Father God, we come to you as humbly as we know how. Lord God, please bless the food and the hands that prepared it. Let no iniquities come into our bodies, in Jesus' name we pray, Amen."

"Amen."

Ham hocks, fried chicken, fatback, corn bread, collard greens, racks of ribs, corn pudding, potato salad, sweet potato pie, lemon pound cake, ice cream and lemonade sat before each of us.

Excited from her outer body experience, Michelle whispered, "Banging on those keys got me hungry."

"Pass the hot sauce, butter and salt, please. No time for all this chatter," Natalia shouted, looking around as if she hadn't eaten in days.

"So, how did you enjoy church, ladies?"

"It was good," they responded as they poked forks down into their food.

Within seconds of eating, I dropped my fork onto the table as if I had seen a ghost. Tommy Lee Davis rolled in the dining area in a wheelchair, spinning around on his own.

Mother Smithfield shouted, "Well, look at God."

"What's wrong, Missy? You look like you've seen a ghost." Michelle was immersed in potato salad and not paying attention to the grand entrance.

I took a deep breath as my arms tingled. "Oh my God!"

The girls looked up and repeated, "Oh my God!"

Michelle observed my behavior and realized I was having an anxiety attack. "Breathe, Missy! Breathe!" She followed my eyes as she noticed I was watching Tommy's every move. "Let's go before you pass out," she said, throwing down her fork onto the purple table cloth.

Natalia rubbed her ear not seeming surprised at all. "What are you talking about? I'm just getting to the point where I'm enjoying the food and fellowship. He ain't nobody to me. I will sit right here and continue to eat."

I put my head down in disbelief and tried to play it off as if I was happy to see him. He rolled over to my table looking glad to see me.

"Three weeks in the hospital and you couldn't come and see me, huh?" He grinned and his brown eyes sparkled.

My hands were shaking. "I was going to call your brother today and arrange a visit."

"Oh, is that so?" He reached out, touching my leg and moving his hand up and down.

"Yes, why would you think otherwise, hun?"

He looked at Natalia and Michelle with labored breath. "I'm sure your girlfriends convinced you to let me rot in that hospital bed alone. Huh?"

Michelle responded abruptly, "Unfortunately, we have nothing to do with her decisions like you assume." While Tommy sat fuming, other church members came over to hug and greet him. They were happy to see him. They lined up one by one to show him love.

Natalia continued to talk under her breathtaking offense of Tommy's last comment. "It's okay, let that yeller punk think what he wants. He ain't nobody to me," Natalia said as she lifted her chicken leg to her mouth.

He waited for the hugs and well wishes to end, then responded, "Punk? Oh, so now we're on name-calling terms?" he asked.

She put her chicken to the side and stood up. "Why not? We had a shooting in the church! Name calling ain't nothing. I advise you to shut that trap before I roll your big apple head ass out of here."

"Okay, okay, stop it you two. No cursing in the church, so embarrassing! Oh my God! This is supposed to be a happy occasion, right? He is alive and he came in healthy and still looking good. Let me finish up here, Tommy, and I'll get with you in a few minutes."

"All right. Don't have me waiting too long." He spun his chair around as if he had been riding in one for a long time and headed toward the door. Natalia clawed at the air making an attempt to snatch him back. We shoved her shoulders and pushed her back down in the chair. "Count to ten, girl, and stop acting ignorant in the church house."

She pumped her fist. "I'm not acting any different than he is if you ask me. He came in here looking for a fight."

"No, he didn't. You've just got pent-up anger," I said as my heart raced.

"This pent-up anger could really help you if you let it. Say the word and I will do what the shooter didn't do."

Michelle began to gather our things. "Let's go, ladies! I can't deal."

I got up from the table and walked toward Tommy as he waited for a plate of food. "It's almost as if you're a living miracle. I don't understand how you got shot six times and you're sitting here in front of me."

"Six shots were fired but only two hit me, hun. You would know that if you came to see me. God isn't ready for me yet." He smirked.

"I bet he isn't." I looked down, assessing his wheelchair Cadillac on fake 22's.

"I can walk a little, it's just easier to use this chair when trying to get around in this big church. Stop looking at me like I'm paralyzed."

He grabbed my hand. "Can I come and see you tonight?"

"I'll call you in a few hours and let you know. Not for sure if I have another service to attend this evening." I crossed my fingers while lying.

"Okay, then."

I bent down to hug him. "I need to catch up with the girls."

"Okay, see you later."

I ran outside with the girls and said, "Oh Lord, what am I going to do now?" I shrugged, feeling confused.

"You are going to continue to pray and ask God to guide you. You really care for Beanie, remember, not Tommy. Don't mess a good thing up for Mt. Zion's jerk of the year." Michelle rubbed my back trying to calm me down.

"He'd better be glad I didn't have my pocket knife or else—"

I stopped Natalia in the middle of her sentence as my hand rose up to her face. "Let's stop all the violent comments, please. This is the house of God, for Christ's sake."

We walked silently to our cars, still in disbelief of the unexpected visitor. We hugged one another as we all stood with a worried look.

Michelle whispered in my ear, "Be strong, my friend. You are too blessed to be stressed about all of this."

I smiled as I opened my car door. I slumped in the seat, feeling droplets of sticky perspiration trickle down my back while the girls got in their cars and drove away. A cascade of thoughts ran through my head as a loud thump sounded at my window.

"Roll down the window, gal."

My dad looked down at me as I rolled the window down two inches. "Yes, sir?"

"Now I know you didn't let that yeller negro run you out of the church dinner. Rushing out just because he arrived was not a good look."

The scent of his cologne tickled my nose. "Daddy, I can't sit in there with that man all up under me. What was I supposed to do?"

"Ignore him and sit right there. You have to show church folks you ain't fazed by him. You can't let him get to you like that."

THAT CHURCH LIFE

"Oh, like you showed the church when you married Sylvia instead of your real baby momma, Olivia?" I put my hands on my hips now ready to take on whatever he had to say about the matter. My eyebrows caved in as if I dared him to tell me a lie.

"Huh?"

"Yeah, huh what?"

"Olivia. I haven't heard that name in over twenty years. Who you been talking to, gal?"

"She came to see me personally! And you want to talk about showing people strength, huh?"

He lifted his hand up as if he was going to slap me dead in the mouth for talking back. "Watch your tone, gal?"

"For what? What you gonna do? Put me across your knee and spank me?" I braced myself, counting down for his hand to reach my face.

He tapped his thumb on the roof of the car and yelled, "Get out of the car and come into my office, now. You ain't never too grown to get a whoopin'! You hear me, gal?" I didn't move and sat still with my arms folded. He tapped the window again. "If I have to repeat myself it will not be a good day for you, Minister Missy Jones!"

I opened the car door slowly and looked away. I was so disappointed and could not look him in the eye. I walked behind him, kicking the pebbles in the parking lot in front of me, scraping my purple stilettos. I wanted to shake him for lying to me all of these years.

We entered the church through the back door as he mumbled to himself. We entered his study as I shoved the door behind us.

He leaned over on his desk. "Now let's get something straight, young lady. As long as you are a child of God, you'd better not *ever* raise your voice at me again. You hear me, gal?"

I put my head down, assessing the scuff on my new shoes. "Yes, sir."

"Now, let's get to the heart of the matter, shall we?" He sat down in his maroon leather chair, designed for his big and tall frame, and swirled it around. He crossed his fingers and sat up straight as if he was ready to strike a new business deal. "Well, speak now or forever hold your peace, gal."

"Olivia came to see me. She showed me a birth certificate and some pictures. How could you keep something so important away from me?" I asked as I hit my hand on his desk.

He looked down, smacking his lips and said, "Because I love you, that's how. Olivia was into all kinds of stuff, chile. She used drugs, slept with lots of men, sold her body for chump change, crazy stuff. I was young and didn't know what to do when she told me she was pregnant. Once you came out of her womb, I had to make sure that you belonged to me. I was happy that a child from my loins had been created. But I knew I had to be married. I just picked the wrong person to fall in love with. You know the church would not have accepted her along with my sins."

I cleared my throat, trying to speak in a low tone. "So aren't you in the saving soul business? You couldn't work with her?"

"See, that's why you are in the mess that you're in. You can't always strive to change folks who don't want to be changed. Olivia was determined to do what she wanted to do and left you behind many nights while she ran the streets. I didn't need all that in my life."

I shook my head, remaining quiet for a few minutes, tapping my toe on the floor. My eyes felt sore as I rubbed away more tears. "I guess there is nothing else to say now that the cat is out of the bag, huh?"

"Missy, you were better off without her, trust me. I chose Sylvia to be my wife because I knew she would love you and care for you as her own. She was a good woman and she loved you so much. I wouldn't have it any other way." He stood up and stretched out his arms. "Come here, gal. Get yourself together and straighten up your face. I did everything I could to protect you and your name." He hugged me tightly.

"Yeah, I know."

"You're blessed! Don't look at all of this as something bad. God loved you so much that he gave you a nurturing mother. In return, she gave you everything you ever wanted and needed. Olivia only played church, she didn't care for the church. She didn't even love me enough to change her wicked ways." His voice heightened. "You wait till I see her, though. I got something for her. She done waited all these years to come down here and disturb the peace. Who does that?"

"Who does that?" I laughed loudly. "Aren't you becoming hip to the twenty-first century slang. But seriously, don't be mad at her, Daddy. Maybe she's at the point of her life where she's trying to make everything right. All we can do is pray that she gets it together before the good Lord takes her away from this world."

"I might take her out before he does, ole—"

"Daddy, stop. Obviously, there was something about her that made you lay down with her."

He stretched his eyes. "It is well within my soul then. I loved Sylvia too much to go back that far in my memory bank. I want to remember the good times with Sylvia instead of remembering the bad times with that do-nothing Olivia."

I turned to the door. "All right, I need to get out of here before Tommy finds out that I'm still on the premises."

"You trying to avoid him? You feeling all right?"

"Yes, I'm fine. It took me a long time to see the light but God is working on me."

"Well thanks be to God to whom all blessings flow!" He followed me to the door. "'I'm going to keep praying for your Boaz, gal."

I began to reach for the doorknob and responded, "God is blessing me more than you know, Daddy."

He looked up, throwing his hands in the air as if he was giving God a praise. "Lord, you are so good to me. I feel like dancing on that one," he said as he chuckled.

I left out feeling better. I was glad that I released my feelings to my father. I loved my current circle of life and now I had to decide if I wanted Ms. Olivia in it.

Rushing to my car, I had a lot of thinking to do. I was anxious to get home and call Beanie. Tommy was only in my mind as I visualized our breakup conversation.

Chapter 17

Three years ago...

I remember the first time he hit me. We were on our way to the mall. He was irritated that I spent the entire day with my sorority sisters and didn't meet up with him until later that evening.

"I don't know who you think you're dealing with, girl. I come first, you hear me! When you graduate, those chicks won't even remember your name. But I will be here, right by your side. How dare you have me waiting all day!"

"But I told you I was going to be with them most of the day. I don't bother you when you are out with your boys."

"What did you just say to me?"

As we drove down Martin Luther King Jr. Drive, he went on and on about how I disrespected him. Before I could get a word out of my mouth in rebuttal, he hit me in it. His hand scraped against my front teeth, ripping off his skin. I reached over and hit him right back as the sting of my hand made him swerve near the sewage drain on the side of the road. This was my first time being hit by a man. It was the first of many. But I never backed down and I always fought back.

THAT CHURCH LIFE

I watched the gleam of the sunshine pierce through my bedroom window as I rolled over on my right side. Last night's conversation with my dad uplifted my soul. I should have gone to him in the beginning instead of talking to Mother Smithfield. I felt good about knowing that someone loved me that much to save me from a life of hardship with an unfit mother.

I stretched and moved his hand from behind me. Now, his soft touch was against my abdomen.

Why did I open the door last night? I felt so desperate. Why do I allow him to have so much power over me?

After all the trash talking, I realized that Tommy Lee Davis was an illicit drug that I consumed daily. I had to have him, I was a fiend for his touch. His seduction was incomparable. Lord, get me out of this!

He lifted his head, still smelling like day-old Polo cologne. "Good morning, beautiful."

"Good morning." I smiled sheepishly.

He played in my hair as he reached over to ask, "What's for breakfast?"

I closed my eyes, not inclined to move from my position. He shouldn't be here, but I felt obligated to show some form of attention. The shooting crossed my mind over and over again. I was glad that the shooter was finally caught and we could lay here fearless without worrying about him coming after Tommy again. "Call Lola; she can fix you some breakfast," I responded back in a soft, playful tone.

I wanted to get to the bottom of why Lola had reappeared in his life.

"I haven't been around Lola for a long time. I can't explain why that dude came at me like that. You believe me, don't you?"

Shaking my head from side to side, I told him, "No. Not at all."

He lifted his head surprised at my curt response. "Well, I guess I'm just going to show you instead of tell you. How about we meet up with Lola, so you can hear it from the horse's mouth?"

I punched the pillow. "Are you kidding me? I'm not sure that's a good idea considering our history. After our altercation last year, I don't think I can sit still when she's being facetious."

"Well, you handled your own when she stepped to you last time."

My mind suddenly returned to that moment not long ago.

The very first year in this relationship, Miss Lola came to me after a Fifth Sunday Jubilee ready for an explanation on my role in Tommy's life. She heard that I was Tommy's girl and didn't understand how that was even possible when he informed her that she was the only one for him.

Instead of causing a major scene, I simply said, "Let's handle this later. This is not the time nor place." She agreed and after church she suggested that we sit down and talk about it at her house to clear the air. I followed her home after service, jumped out of the car, and without allowing her to say one word, I fought her like a man with professional boxing skills in her own front yard. If it wasn't for her neighbor coming outside to break us apart, I think I would have taken her life.

Tommy rolled over on top of me looking straight into my eyes. He lifted up as if he was about to do a set of pushups. "I want you to think about it for a few days," he said, picking up my cell phone off the dresser to check the time. "I see you have a few voicemails waiting."

"Okay. And?"

"You seem defensive. All I said was you have a few voicemails."

"What are you saying then?" I sat up ready for an argument.

"I'm not trying to say a thing. You okay?"

"I will be okay when you stop accusing me of stuff."

"I have yet to accuse you of anything. But since you brought it up, you got some other nigga calling you?"

"None of your doggone business."

I crawled under his arms and moved to my side of the bed. "Sounds like you might be a little jealous or worried."

"Oh trust me, it doesn't matter. I'm not worried. I know who has your heart and it ain't that nigga you hollering at, that's for sure."

The nerve of this dude speaking as if he had me wrapped around his finger and I would never leave him. This late-night rendezvous was definitely a mistake and I could now see why Michelle told me to seek help. I had lost my mind.

I was all riled up pushing covers off my legs now ready to punch him in his left eye. "I think you should go." I pointed to the door, hoping he would exit immediately.

"Huh? We haven't spent time together in weeks. What did I do?"

"Not enough to stay in my bed and eat my food, that's for sure. I think you should go. I don't think we can continue like this." I pulled the covers off of him waiting for him to get out of my bed.

"What the hell do you mean, Missy? I see right now your good sense left your brain. Are you dumping me?"

With my hand on my chin, I answered, "Why yes. I'm glad you figured it out on your own. You're so smart." I closed my eyes and cringed, trying to ignore his hand rubbing up and down my leg.

He kissed my belly and said, "I'm not going anywhere. Believe that!"

"Last time I checked, you don't pay my bills. It's time for you to get out of my house and leave me alone for good. This was all a big mistake."

"Who you think gonna put up with your church fanatical ways? You better be glad you're a freak in the bedroom or else I would have walked away a long time ago." He pulled his hand away as he looked for his pants.

"Oh, so I am a church fanatic, huh?"

He rolled his eyes. "More like a Jesus freak."

"Well, you liked it!" I yelled as I gathered the rest of his things and threw them at the front door. "Thanks for wasting the last five years of my life, creep. Now get out!"

"It's been my pleasure to serve that big booty. You will never find another like me, woman. Trust and believe!"

I threw my shoe at him as he bent down to get the rest of his things. He stood up limping as he charged me and pinned me down on the bed.

I threw my legs up trying to break free. "Cheater! I guess you have to pin me down so I can't whoop your tail!"

He balled his fist up and put it in my face. "Keep talking and I swear I will shove that shoe down your throat, preacher girl."

I tussled, trying to push him to the other side of the bedroom. I knew he didn't have the strength or stamina to handle me. I snatched my alarm clock and threw it at him. "All this time I've been lying, telling people how I started all the fights. Well now I can tell them the truth! You ain't man enough to stand up to men, instead you love pounding your fists on women, punk!"

"I got your punk. If you ever come out your mouth to those church folks, I swear I will—"

"What? Do what? I dare you to put your hands on me ever again!" I punched him in his chest right where fresh bandages wrapped around to his back.

He squealed, bending in pain as he swung at the air. Instead of connecting his punches, he landed on the floor, lying on his stomach.

"You're gonna pay for this, hoe. You just wait until I get myself together."

"Nigga, you ain't never been together with your leeching self. Get out of my house before I call the police. Fix it, Jesus!"

"Typical church girl, act like the devil all night long and then call on Jesus in the morning. I got something for you. Just wait. When I heal, you better watch your back."

"Boy, do you know who I am? You better watch yours!" My index finger in the air, I screamed, "Now get out!"

He grabbed the bed linen for assistance. He stood straight up with his fingers formed like a trigger. He used his other hand and held his chest as blood spurted out of the bandages, "All right, I will leave you alone. By the way, I was screwing Lola. I lied!"

"Duh. The whole world knows that, fool. Now get out!"

He stumbled to the door, turned around and said, "Now take that one for the church team."

My forehead wrinkled. I picked up a broom and shoved him out the door with the broomstick touching his backside.

For the first time I didn't cry. Instead of tears, my eyes were filled with blotches of red and full of anger. "Don't let me see you in the street, punk!" I yelled as I slammed my door.

THAT CHURCH LIFE

My phone kept ringing, but I didn't answer it at first. I tried to catch my breath before doing that. I should have choked him out. I probably would have felt better afterwards.

I stretched my hands to reach the cell phone. "Hello."

"Hey, me lady, did I catch you at a bad time?"

I sat down trying to talk in a normal tone. "No, not at all. How are you?"

"I can't complain, I would be better if you were here with me."

Too tired to respond, I sat in disbelief and paused.

"Is everything okay, me lady? You're mighty quiet."

"Everything is fine. I just had a real extensive workout, that's all." God knows I did. "I miss you."

"I miss you, too, love. I will be in the States next week to visit my sister in New York. I want to drive down to North Carolina after our visit. Can I come and see you?"

My eyes lifted up to the ceiling. Thank you, Jesus! A quick turnaround from what just happened. I bounced off the bed with excitement. "That would be wonderful. What day are you coming?"

"Oh, probably Friday or Saturday and leave out Sunday evening if that's okay?"

I squirmed. Coming to church with me, already! "Um Yeah, that sounds good."

"All right, me lady. I will call you when I reach the North

Carolina line. Miss you much."

"Ditto!"

"See you soon."

"Okay, bye."

I rushed to the bathroom to empty my bladder and examine my face for scratches. I wanted to make sure he didn't leave bruises during the fifty-sixth round of our WWF Wrestling match.

All I could think about was how I could get back at him for all the trouble and heartache he had caused me. Beanie would want to attend church and hopefully Tommy would be in place to play the organ.

I bet that would eat him up. Lord, be with me. I ran out of the bathroom holding my hand over my mouth as I plopped on the bed. I put the phone up to my ear and tried to call Olivia again. No answer and it went straight to voicemail. I prayed before leaving a message.

Dear Lord, only you can set me free.

Cover me.

Guide me.

Wash me.

Cleanse me.

In Jesus' name.

THAT CHURCH LIFE

Chapter 18

Sitting at my desk at work, I listened to the rain hit the roof with force. It was a dreary and long day, but I challenged myself to complete a full eight hours. It had been several days since the big fall out with Tommy and I was actually glad that I ended the relationship. Now I felt calm and somewhat normal. It was that time of the week to have a conference call with my girls.

"Hello?"

"Hey! Hold on let me get Natalia on the line."

"Hello?"

"Hey there. It's Missy and Michelle. I have you on conference mode."

"What's up, ladies?" Natalia screamed.

I smiled, "Nothing much on my end. Back at work."

Michelle jumped in, "I bet you are hating that right now."

"Yes, ma'am. I really need my own business."

Michelle cleared her throat. "When you become that big time pastor, you won't have to worry about that job anymore."

"So you must have something important to talk about. Anytime you put us on a conference call, we get an ear full from you. Go ahead and spill it all, Missy," Natalia said.

I closed my eyes and put the phone up close to my ear as I dreaded telling them the story. "Umm, well. Tommy came to my house the night of the Jubilee."

With a gasp, Michelle said, "Oh my, here we go! Drama!"

"Yes, the night was filled with drama. He stayed the night and the next morning the light bulb in my head went off. I got angry thinking about everything and I put him out."

"Do tell!" Natalia mumbled.

"Now, I know the two of you are probably disappointed in my decision to let him back in my house, but I promise you that I am done with him for good this time."

With a long yawn, Michelle said, "I'll believe it when I see it, honey. How many times have we heard that same line from you?"

"I am so serious this time, though. We had a little tussle after I threw a shoe at him."

"Let me guess what comes next, you hit him first and that's why he struck back, right?" Natalia said with sarcasm.

"Okay, this isn't a 'let's gang up on Missy today' session. This was supposed to be a come clean with my girls as I acknowledged my issues."

"Yeah, we get it. That's a great accomplishment when you can be true to yourself and realize that something has to give with your situation. Don't listen to Natalia, you know she's judgmental."

"Judgmental? No, I'm just real. He should have been gone out of her life after the first two months of dating!"

"Well, he wasn't, so as a friend, you need to be more compassionate and helpful. You know Missy suffers from all kinds of anxiety disorders, so why go there?"

"All right you two. I don't need another intervention. Nor do I need my mental health issues exposed! I'm just letting you know my progress. On a better note, Beanie is coming down after visiting his sister in New York this weekend to see me!"

"That's great! I know you're excited to see him. Oh, I'm so happy for you, girl!" Michelle squealed.

"Yeah, great!" Natalia said with minimal enthusiasm.

"I hope everything goes well. I'm a little nervous about bringing him to church with me. I know Tommy is going to flip! And by the way, I've been delivered from my anxiety issues!"

People had been talking about me since I was a child concerning my anxiety. When I was nine years old, the doctors said I suffered from Panic Disorder and Social Phobia. I had a hard time in school dealing with being judged by other children and always held my chest when feeling overwhelmed. My dad kept me in therapy for years. Finally, at the age of twenty-seven, I had learned to cope with some but not all of my barriers that cause my attacks. The good times with

Tommy had me feeling fulfilled and the attacks were not frequent. The bad times, however, always had me in the hospital as these issues overpowered me.

"The devil is a lie," Natalia said.

"You would say that. Anyway, the next time he comes for me, he might have more than two bullets in his chest. I'm just saying."

We all laughed. "Well, thanks for the update, lady. Sorry if I seemed judgmental. I just want the best for you.

"Wow, really? That was nice of you to say, Natalia!"

"Yes, I try to be nice sometimes."

"All right, ladies. It's been a pleasure chatting with you. I will update you on my visit with Mr. Beanie sometime next week."

"That will work," Natalia responded.

"Sounds good to me," Michelle said.

"All right, talk to you later."

I hung up the phone. I finally had the opportunity to show my friends that God was still in the miracle business. It was a sheer miracle to move on with my life. I made a vow to myself and the Lord that after the fight, I would speak life into my situations and really follow God's plan that he had for me.

The end! I could not allow a man such as Tommy to mess up my blessings and destroy my ministry. Nah, I had too much to live for.

I smiled as God spoke to me. "You were made for this."

THAT CHURCH LIFE

Chapter 19

After a quiet evening reading the bible and playing with my cat, I fell asleep on my couch. I woke up with food on the brain. I felt like eating a healthy breakfast and drinking a rich cup of hazelnut coffee with flavored creamer to wash it down. I bent forward to say a quick morning prayer. I was ready to start my day.

I spent a lot of time counting down the days, hours, minutes and seconds until Beanie's arrival. Lots of praying and talking to the Master on giving me the strength to sustain abstinence and remain focused on doing God's work. I was sure people were talking and by now even Mother Smithfield knew about the breakup with Tommy.

The weeping willow tree beside my living room window stood strong and tough as it supplied the right amount of shade needed for a good morning breeze and comfort. I opened my window to obtain some air. The twigs touched my window pane looking sturdy enough to swoop me closer to the sky. A tree such as this was known to endure any kind of weather. It remained tall, no matter the challenge. This was a good tree to have hanging before me. I wished I could imitate its characteristics. Sturdy, strong, tough and long lasting. All the qualities I needed to endure this breakup. I knew it had to happen but I wished it could have ended on better terms. Now more than ever, I needed my daddy's help. I wasn't in denial of that. If he could counsel others in the congregation, then he could help me, too. Being my biological parent and also my pastor made it difficult to take advantage of his expertise in life. But right now, I needed a true shepherd of the Lord to give me a word that would help me to stay free. I picked up the phone and said, "Siri, call my dad."

She responded, "Calling your dad now."

"Hello?"

"Hello, Daddy."

"My Marvelous Missy. How are you, gal?"

I looked out the window. "I'm good."

"Okay, what's wrong? I can hear it in your voice."

Hesitating, I finally said, "Can we get together for breakfast before I go to work?"

"Aw, you need your daddy, don't you? My big baby." He chuckled.

"Yes, very much so. Can you meet me at the IHOP near Costco in a few minutes?"

"Sure, sweetie. I would love to sit down and talk with you. No work today?"

"No, working from home."

"Okay, I will see you in fifteen minutes then."

Happy thoughts.

I shook my head trying to separate the negative from the positive and focus only on productive thinking. "Praying for a new journey in relationships," I said while looking down at my cat. "One day, I will receive a great release and be totally free. One day."

I threw my strapless blue sundress over my head and stepped into my pink and blue slip-on sandals. I grabbed the lotion bottle and massaged lotion on to my legs and feet then pulled my hair back into a bun as I headed out.

I arrived at the restaurant twenty minutes later and tipped into the front lobby as Daddy stood up, already waiting for me. He had on his favorite brown and beige suit looking down at his phone.

"What you doing, old man? Playing Candy Crush?"

"Aww, there she is. Miss North Carolina!" Daddy's voice boomed when he turned around.

I felt comforted with his big hands around my back. Only a true father figure could make his child cheese so hard. "Hi there, Daddy. You are looking sharp. What's the occasion?"

"I had to put on my good suit. I have mission work to do with the elderly unit team today. You want to join us?"

Blinking my eyes in non-interest, I said, "Nah, I'm good."

"So, I guess greeting me with open arms means you feel better after our conversation, huh?" he asked, looking over for an answer.

"Yes. I'm not mad at you anymore. I just wished someone would have told me earlier in life about my mom."

"Now let's be honest here, do you think ten years ago you could have accepted the fact that Sylvia was not your biological mother?"

I twisted my lip. "You're right. Probably not," I said as I smirked, looking into his big gray eyes.

"So, what you been up to?"

I looked down at my sandals. "Well…"

"Oh Lord, it's always something, ain't it?"

My eyes lit up. I was excited to tell him about Beanie. "I met someone while in Jamaica." I showed all my teeth. "He is smart, saved and very kind."

"You don't say." Rubbing his chin, he added, "You never had one like that!"

"Hush, Daddy. He will be in the States in a few days and he will also join me for church on Sunday to hear me preach."

He leaned back on the wall. "Well, that's all right, right there. You do a background check yet?" he asked as his hands waved in the air.

I laughed loudly as the people next to us turned around. "No, I haven't done a background check yet, Daddy. But I'm sure if he isn't right for me, the Holy Ghost will give a signal."

"Yeah, you didn't listen to the Holy Ghost when it came to Tommy. 'Cause I know you had all the signs needed to walk away from that nut. I hope you listen this time around!" He gritted his teeth and asked, "He got all his teeth?"

Laughing loudly again, I told him, "Yes."

"Any children?"

"No."

"Six wives in Africa?"

I shook my head. "No."

"Well, he sounds all right then."

A lady walked to the waiting area and yelled, "Jones, party of two!"

"Right here, ma'am.
"Follow me, please," she said.

We sat in a booth ready to place our order. "What are you having, ma'am?"

"I would like your all-you-can-eat pancake special, please, with bacon on the side."

"All right, how about you, sir?"

"Give me the senior special with extra cheese."

She scribbled on her notepad. "Anything to drink?"

"We will both have some of your good ole coffee and a cup of water, please." Daddy grinned while looking at the waitress' legs as she walked off.

I reached over and shook him back to life. "Daddy, stop staring!"

"Lord have mercy. I wish I had some biscuits to sop her up with and molasses on the side."

I pointed my finger in his face. "Pastor Jones, get your mind out of the gutta."

"I may be old but I shole' ain't dead." He chuckled and his belly moved up and down with his tie flapping around his neck. He got himself together and leaned over with a serious expression.

"So, the question is, are *you* happy?"

"I think so, Daddy. I finally ended it with Tommy and I think I'm moving in the right direction."

His eyes enlarged two times their size. "Oh really, when did this happen?"

"The other night he came over to my house after the Jubilee. I felt stupid for falling for his charm again."

He reached over and grabbed my hand. "Chile, that's what love does to some folks. One minute you're confused, next minute you have starry eyes, next minute you want to kill him. We have all been through it. I'm glad you're moving forward because I have been waiting to have this conversation with you."

"What is it?" I asked as the waitress stepped up to pour our coffee.

"I'm ready for you to start preaching more often so I can move into retirement." His eyes gleamed as he waited for my reaction.

"As in become the pastor at Mt. Zion?"

"Yes, chile. I know you can do it. The people respond to you well and I think you would make a great televangelist. You know what to say and when to say it." He paused. "I wish Mama was still here to see all of this." He looked down as if he was trying not to get emotional. "She would be proud of the third generation Jones girl making progress in the pulpit."

"Yeah, that is kind of amazing in so many ways. But I don't know if I'm ready for that, Daddy. I already have a hard time dealing with church folk now."

He looked up, blinking. "Chile, you're the perfect person to deal with them. You have a great testimony. You are doing better with your anxiety, you removed that rascal Tommy out of your life, you got a college degree even after dealing with an abusive boyfriend, you're getting more focused on the church and you have a good heart for the people even after all that. People can relate to some of the things you have been through. Now I'm going to need you to get some strength and carry on the family legacy."

Our food arrived and the savory smell of the bacon hit my nose instantly. "I'm so hungry. I've been dreaming about a good meal."

"Now that you've decided to leave that yella nigga alone, I can find another musician, right?"

"Yes, sir."

"Ain't no need in him gawking at you in the pulpit while he trying to play."

"Yeah, you're right." I looked around attempting to dismiss the thought of Tommy leaving the church. "When will you tell him to leave? The choir will be fine with Michelle playing. We just need to give them the heads up on the change."

Daddy took his fork and poked his sunny-side up eggs. "They will live. I'm pretty sure we can get Michelle to come back on a permanent basis if the price is right."

I smiled. "I would love to see Michelle back on the organ! Don't remember what we fell out about to make her leave in the first place."

"Yeah, I can't go back that far myself with that one," he replied as he cleared his throat.

I gagged, then coughed as a piece of pancake went down the wrong pipe.

"You okay, gal?"

"Yes, sir."

"Well, whatever was the reason she left, I hope we can keep her this time. With her talent and your vocals, the two of you can bring the house down every Sunday."

"Amen to that."

We finished our meal and walked slowly to our cars as we enjoyed spending time together. I had a lot to think about. New relationship, new duties and a new musician. Too much to swallow in one day. God always made sure he was glorified even in our mess. I was so glad he still trusted me to lead his people and give a word. It was funny how things turned around once you left it in God's hands. I was no longer worried nor did I feel anxious as I leaped into my car grinning. Me, the new pastor? It felt so right.

God, you are awesomely, awesome, in your awesomeness!

THAT CHURCH LIFE

"I will call you later, Daddy!" I yelled before closing my car door.

"All right, gal, you be safe now, ya hear."

"I'm going over to the church to clean the office." I shimmied my shoulders. "Decorate how you want it and we will make the announcement Sunday morning, if you're ready."

"Sunday?"

"Why not? Ain't no time better than the present, right?"

"Oh, okay, well, I will be on my way then. Let me sleep on all of this."

"That might be a good idea. But I tell you what? I bet you will rest easy now. God has worked it all out, chile."

I rolled down the window further to continue. "Thank you for a wonderful breakfast, Daddy. I will start moving things around slowly. I have to get used to all of this, you know."

Daddy started singing, "You got a blessing with your name on it. Ha, sing it with me, you're blessed, blessed, blessed, blessed. Get ready, get ready, it's your time, daughter!"

Chapter 20

I drove down to the church with the intent of fixing my new office and cleaning up decorations that were left from the Fifth Sunday Jubilee service. I entered the building, and right before shutting the front door, I heard a car enter the parking lot. I looked up and it was Olivia pulling up in a blue minivan.

I left the door open for her. I was eager to hear what she had to say this time around. A part of me wanted to know more but another part of me wanted her to disappear and go back to California.

She walked swiftly to the church's doorstep. She realized the door was cracked for her to enter and walked right inside with a bounce. She had a smug look as if something was bothering her. She realized after taking off her sunglasses that I was standing in the hallway waiting for her to enter. The weather's forecast was for warm temperatures and sunny skies with expected showers in the afternoon. But the rain came early for me as her wrinkled face showed me that she was not happy to see me.

"Hello, Olivia."

"Hello!" she replied as I reached for a hug. "So happy to see you, my daughter."

I rolled my eyes and folded my arms knowing that was not the truth. She had been in North Carolina for weeks and never returned any of my calls as I tried desperately to get more information about her past. "Why are you still in the city? I thought you would be long gone by now considering you haven't answered any of my phone calls."

She stepped in the center of the hallway flinging her purse over her shoulder. "No, I decided to stay in North Carolina for a while since it's so expensive to go back and forth to California."

"I see," I said as I tapped my foot like a school teacher feeling annoyed.

Her eyes raced as she tried to peek in the sanctuary through the hallway wooden doors. "May I go in?"

I hesitated and answered looking down. It wasn't in my blood to be mean to her, so I said, "Sure."

She entered and looked up at the high ceilings and then over to the stained-glass windows. "This is a nice church. I'm very impressed. Did it always look this way?"

"No, we made upgrades several years ago. How did you know that I would be here, Ms. Olivia?"

She spun around quickly. "Actually, I didn't know. I was looking for your father this time."

"Oh." I stood still with a blank stare, still not giving her any info.

"So where is your father?" She looked around as if he was hiding somewhere in the sanctuary.

"Um, he isn't here just yet… Can we cut to the chase?" I asked. "Because I have a lot of things to do. You haven't returned any of my calls so it's clear you aren't really trying to get to know your daughter. What do you want?"

Her eyes turned red as she rolled them looking as if she was trying to hold back tears from not responding to my calls. She swung her purse in the air and shouted, "I want my money that is owed to me."

I was perplexed by her statement. "What money?"

"Your daddy verbally promised that if I walked away from being your mother, he would pay me. We agreed that I couldn't lay eyes on you until after the age of twenty-six. You are twenty-seven now, right? I want my one hundred thousand dollars for my pain and suffering or some heads will roll."

"Pain and suffering? You had pain and suffering? You could have said *no* to that agreement. You chose to suffer!" I hissed at such nonsense. "You didn't have to raise me, you lived your life in peace, and no one bothered you for anything! You've got some nerve, lady!"

Her voice went an octave higher. "Shame on you! It was hard to give you up contrary to your beliefs. I cried for years."

I leaned to the side with my arms still folded. "Yeah right. From the looks of it, you sure didn't mind being without me, ma'am."

THAT CHURCH LIFE

She grabbed my arm, swinging me around in a circle and pushed me against the back pew. She was strong for such a little woman and handled me with great force.

"Look here. I have done everything that was asked of me and I want my damn money. You hear me?" She shook her finger in my face as she pushed me further onto the wooden frame. "Don't make me go public, you spoiled brat. I will bring this entire church organization down to its knees. I didn't answer your calls because I don't have anything to say to you. You are right, I don't care nothing about you or your father and his reputation. I just want my money and I want it sooner than later. You hear me, little heifer?"

Mother Smithfield was right!

"I got your heifer, you whore!" I leaned forward, pushing her off of me. "I didn't make a money deal with you, he did! So you need to find him and make it his problem, not mine!" I jerked my body completely away. "Now get your mooching tail out before this here heifer calls the police!"

She threw her hand up in the air and said, "This entire operation will be mine, sweetie, all mine." Her face was smug and her eyes were daunting.

She walked out, slamming the front door. I stood speechless and contemplated on beating her down in the church parking lot. Did Daddy just make me pastor so that he wouldn't have to forfeit the church?

I pulled my cell phone out of my purse, pressing the numbers with great pressure.

"Hello?"

"Daddy, really? Did you make me pastor so that you wouldn't lose the church?"

He paused and took a deep breath before answering. "Who told you such a thing?"

"Daddy, don't play with me. Did you make an agreement with Olivia?"

He began to stutter, "Back then I didn't have a choice."

"Lies. We all have choices, Daddy. You chose to use your own daughter as a pawn to get back at her and you know it!"

"Missy, I didn't mean any harm. I meant every word I said to you earlier. It's time! You are ready to go forth and be the leader that God has called you to be in spite of Olivia showing her face. I was preparing to retire any day now. With Olivia showing back up in Durham, it just made it easier to move forth. I had to do what I had to do."

"I am so tired of you and your sick twisted mind games! So you think me being the pastor is going to stop her from suing you? Did you sign any paperwork with this woman?"

"Yes…" He paused with a long sigh.

THAT CHURCH LIFE

"Why would you do such a thing, Daddy?" I walked around stomping my feet as my anxiety escalated faster than a rocket shooting to the moon.

"I don't want to lose the church. My mother worked too hard for us to lose the church over a bad decision I made years ago. Our members would be devastated if they found out I lost the church all because I had a baby mama that I was trying to make stay hidden for twenty-seven years."

"You are just trying to appease these church folks? That's all you care about, what people think." I gripped the phone tightly. "Let her have it all if she wants it. Don't use me in your mess!"

"Honey, I am not using you. I am protecting you and the family legacy. I don't want that old trick to take down what we have worked so hard to build. Our name is all we got. In the paperwork I signed, it stated that if you became the next living heir of the church, she could not take the building and I would only owe her the cash amount promised."

I sat in silence blowing out heavy volumes of air. I ran up and down the church aisle in full rage. I kicked my shoes off and threw them in across the 6,500-square-foot floor. They landed in the missionary section making a loud thump on the linoleum floor. If I had my way, I would have turned over every pew in the room. Luckily, the pews were nailed to the floor which didn't allow me to do much damage. I felt like I couldn't breathe. "I don't have any words for you right now, Pastor Henry Jones. I am so hurt right now!"

"Missy, I need you to calm down before you get yourself sick again. Now is not the time to be laying up in the hospital. I need you ready to preach the next Sunday sermon without any interruptions. Sleep on it and we will talk in the morning."

I pressed the red disconnect button on my cell phone to intentionally drop the call. I was infuriated with the lies and deceit of my own father and threw the phone onto the ground. He raised me to be honest and humble and here he was acting like a pure demon. Too upset to fathom the outcome, one thing was for sure; Ms. Olivia Wallace wasn't getting jack! I didn't care about the family name. I cared about getting back at her for giving me up for money and church property. Not only would I run this church and bring it up to date with twenty-first century practices, but I would also show the world that God had given me the power to do it all. I would lose my life before allowing this stranger to take over everything. Ms. Olivia would be put in her place, for good!

THAT CHURCH LIFE

Chapter 21

It was Saturday, the day my Beanie man was expected to pass the green and white *Welcome to North Carolina* sign thirty miles outside of Warren County. After visiting family in New York, he was ecstatic about making that ten-hour drive to visit my church and home. He called every other hour just to say how much he missed me.

Between phone calls, I called all board members to attend an emergency meeting. The board needed to be kept abreast of everything. They also needed to meet and greet their new pastor. I planned to talk about the changes that would be made throughout the church. I wondered how they would feel about my dad switching roles, Tommy being fired and Michelle returning on payroll as a full-time musician. Michelle agreed with returning and accepted our new offer. I thought it would be a good idea to invite her to the meeting and pick her up so that we could kill two birds with one stone. We needed to catch up with everything so that she could talk me through it all.

She braced herself in her seat as I sped away from her home.

"Slow down, girl!"

"Sorry, it's a habit." I looked at the speedometer and realized I was going past forty miles per hour within a residential area.

"Dang! What's the rush?" Michelle looked over at me as her weave flew across her neck line due to the open sunroof.

"I want to hurry up and get this meeting over with so I can meet up with Beanie. We need to go over our new roles with the board. I don't want him waiting on me being in a new town and all."

"My new position? Your new role?" she asked.

"Oh, I didn't tell you? Daddy is making me pastor and he is giving you full-time status on the organ. I know you accepted to come and play for us but we need you to come in as the Music Director. We are firing Tommy and Daddy is ready to retire," I spat.

She looked at me with dreamy eyes as she put her hand on my shoulder. "Wow, that is a blessing! I told you years ago this was your calling."

"Yeah, you always knew what was best for me."

"Now see, that ain't nothing but God! He's setting you up to be pastor and gave you a saved man to go along with your new role. I am so glad God brought the two of you together. You better go and get your blessing, gurl!"

I laughed at her southern drawl. "So, are you ready for every Sunday key playing?"

She hesitated and shook her head. "I guess. I told your father I didn't mind coming back when he hinted to it last Sunday. I don't know, though."

"What's that all about? You guess? You used to love Mt. Zion. It seemed like you was always there practicing more than me."

Looking straight ahead with a blank expression, she said, "One day, I will tell you all about it, my friend. Are you sure you're firing Tommy for good?"

I jerked my neck and took my eyes off the road. I looked over and noticed tears trickling down her fat brown cheeks. "Michelle, are you okay?"

"No! I'm not okay."

"What's wrong?"

She paused, trying to explain in a clear voice, "Returning back to Mt. Zion brings back a lot of memories that I have tried to forget. But I see now I have to be honest with you in order to really overcome this thing."

"What thing?" We came to a stoplight as I grabbed some tissue out of the glove compartment and passed it to her. "Listening to you being real about your situation gave me courage and strength to one day tell my story."

"Well, I hope your story is nothing like my crazy life. I want you to tell me before you share it with the entire church family." I ran my hands across the steering wheel, trying to figure out what could have possibly happened at church. Whatever it was it still filled Michelle with sour feelings after all these years. "Say something, girl."

"Trust me, Missy, you really don't want to know. I was planning to go to my grave with this one." She wiped her nose with the tissue as uncontrollable drainage came down her left nostril. "But now that you are truly moving on with your life, I think you need to know some of this."

"Listen, I think if you come clean about whatever happened to you, it will be easier for me to help you through this. Okay?"

She turned to me and said, "Can you just park the car for a minute?"

"Why?"

"Missy, it's a long story and I don't want you crashing into anyone or anything once I tell you all about it."

When I looked at her, it was as if her face had turned colors. I pulled the car over onto Alston Avenue and pulled into the Burger King parking lot. The car's engine purred when I put it in reverse to back in. I closed the sunroof top and said, "I'm all ears, sweetie. What happened?"

"Promise me you won't get mad at me when I tell you this. And promise me that we will continue to be friends no matter what."

"Oh my, it's something that deep that it could end our friendship? I always thought you left because of our argument about religion and my entry into the ministry."

"Nah, that's far from it, Missy. Do you remember the night I stayed a few minutes late after rehearsal? Tommy was supposed to teach me how to play one of those fast Tye Tribbett songs that you wanted to sing?"

"Yeah, we needed to learn that song for the youth revival that year. What about it?"

She put her face in her hands. "Tommy came on to me."

"Okay, so you think I won't speak to you anymore because of that? You're a beautiful woman. He comes on to everybody!"

Her hands shook. "There's more."

I turned completely around in my seat. "Okay?"

"Tommy could not take no for an answer. He always bragged about how he was going to hit the golden jackpot with all the 'young fresh meat' in church as he called it. After everyone left out of the sanctuary that night, he became very aggressive. He scared me half to death when he grabbed me closer to him each time I said no." She cried uncontrollably recalling the event. "He pulled up my skirt and screamed at me saying I wanted it and why fight it." I gasped.

"I tried hard to push him off of me as he laid me across the piano but being such a tall and strong man, it was almost impossible."

"Oh my God, Michelle!"

"I screamed as loud as I could and no one helped me, no one." She sniffled. "I never wanted to tell you because I knew how you felt about him and knowing that you had just become an ordained minister, I didn't want you to lose your focus." She looked me eye to eye. "Our argument wasn't about your position. I was angry with myself and took it out on you. Our argument sparked from hiding the truth of what happened."

I reached over to hug her. "I am so sorry, sis. I had no idea." I cried along with her. "Why would you keep something like this to yourself after all of these years? You allowed me to be hurt by this dude knowing he did this to you?"

She leaned over and put her head on my shoulder. "I have been getting counseling from your father once a month since the incident happened. He never gave names. I just told him bits and pieces of some of the things I was going through. We would always end up talking about you after each session and how he wanted you to stay focused and move forward in God. I knew this would alter your focus. Now that you are following the path that God has set for your life, I thought I would share this with you."

My heart dropped. "What?" My bottom lip became thin as I bit most of it to prevent from cursing. "Oh my God. You mean to tell me that my father has known about this after all this time and didn't tell me?"

"Don't get mad at him. You know he isn't supposed to tell you confidential information like that. Everyone knew that you were destined for greatness and I didn't want to interfere. I pressed charges against him for statutory rape but he only received probation."

THAT CHURCH LIFE

"Are you okay? I am lost for words." Something was wrong with this story. Did she know Tommy *before* he came to the church in order for it to be statutory rape! Was my sister lying to me?

"Unfortunately, the story isn't over, sis."

I put my hands over my mouth. "No, sis, no…"

"Yes, I became pregnant. I had an abortion."

I started the engine up by pushing the automatic start button and swerved out of the parking lot almost hitting a mother and her children trying to get into the fast food place. I couldn't control my anger as I screamed at the top of my lungs, "Lord, this can't be happening, ugh!"

"Missy, calm down! You are going to get us killed."

I thought about all the beatings I took off that sorry man and now I find out that he raped my best friend. I held onto the steering wheel as tight as I could as I maneuvered the car from lane to lane going in and out of traffic.

Michelle became afraid and held on to the dashboard while pressing her foot down on the floor as if she had a brake on her side of the vehicle.

"Missy, you've got to slow down. Get it together, please, before we both die."

With that statement, I suddenly stopped right in front of the intersection of Liberty Street and Alston Avenue in front of the old sea food restaurant. I jumped out of the car in a rage. I cried and cried as I kicked my leg into the air trying to get some form of satisfaction.

I was too distraught to even look at her as I couldn't even imagine the burden she carried all of these years.

This can't be true. Impossible!

"I'm so sorry, sis. I am so sorry he hurt you." I leaned over on the hood of the car trying hard to calm down.

"I know how it must feel to hear this. This is why everyone, and I do mean everyone, tried getting you away from that sociopath."

"Do any other church members know?"

"No. The only person that knew anything was Pastor Jones and he hasn't told a soul."

"I'm so sorry, sis."

"Stop saying you're sorry. You didn't do anything, *he* did this."

This doesn't sound right at all!

I pounded my fist on the hood. "He will pay for all the pain he has caused. I promise you that."

Michelle opened her car door for air. "It's okay, my friend. It did feel good to finally get it off my chest. I just hope this doesn't bring a wedge between us."

I frowned. "Never! Why would you even think of such a thing?"

"Okay. Just calm down, honey. I'm sure you haven't taken the new medication they gave you in the hospital for that anxiety this morning, have you?"

I looked up again giving her confirmation with my eyes like a guilty child. "No, I haven't. Left my medication on the dresser this morning. But I told you, I've been delivered from that."

She smiled. "See, I know you better than you know yourself. Now get in this car so we can go to the church. We need to get this meeting over with so you can meet up with your boo thang. Maybe a cup of tea will help to calm your nerves."

I walked around the car rubbing the dust off the sides. "I don't know what I was thinking. Why did I stay with that man for so long? I feel like a pile of cow manure." I couldn't put my finger on it but something was terribly wrong. I had to believe what my sister was saying to me. She was my sister and she had always told me the truth.

"We will get through this, sis." Michelle slapped my hand and locked in with my pinky.

"You better know it, girl."

"This too shall pass! Now drive like you got some sense. I'm ready to hear Mother Smithfield's commentary in this meeting. She is going to put everyone in check. She is the Mt. Zion Missionary queen!"

We both laughed, bending over. "Yes, indeed she is." I reached for her hand. "Know that I love you, sis."

She embraced my hand and held it tight. "I love you, too, Missy Rochelle Jones."

Chapter 22

There was never a dull moment during our monthly board meetings. Eight members sat at the oval table placed in the middle of the church conference room. They brought in notebooks, bibles and tape recorders every meeting, to ensure that every resource was available.

Daddy called everyone over the phone to have a conference call on what he planned to discuss. He wanted to alert them all quickly so that they wouldn't be surprised once they came in to discuss things face to face.

When they arrived, they all sat down hurriedly knowing that Daddy didn't want to waste much time since they were familiar with the topics at hand.

"Thanks for showing up at last notice everyone. We are here to discuss my plans to retire and give the ministry to my daughter as head pastor. Also on the agenda, we will talk about Michelle Hanks coming back to her home church as the head musician and dismissing Tommy Lee Davis from his duties. Any questions before we get started?"

"How will the members feel about Missy being the pastor?" Mother Smithfield asked as she swiveled back and forth in her chair.

"I think it will all work out just fine. She is young, vibrant and smart. They love her already so it won't be a hard switch. Don't you think?" Pastor Jones asked.

"I know that smile will bring in a new generation of members, that's for sure!" Mother Taylor said.

"I hope it's not just about a smile. It better be about the word of God!" Daddy said.

Daddy was always annoyed by silly comments by his board members, but he had to deal with them since they were in place before he became the pastor of the church. They did everything to kiss up to him even when he was wrong.

"Michelle, do you mind taking notes for us, please since our secretary isn't here yet?"

She smiled and said, "Sure thing, Pastor Jones."

"We need to come together and make sure that we have open arms for all these new ideas," Deacon Freemon said, looking over at Sister Mary's slit in her skirt.

"Amen," Sister Mary said, batting her eyes.

"We can't put things in place and not support it one hundred percent, regardless of what we used to do. It's time for a change," Pastor Jones noted with authority.

"Let's make the motion that Missy is our new pastor effective next Sunday!" Mother Smithfield shouted. She wanted this board meeting to be short. The bingo table was waiting for her arrival.

Deacon Freemon couldn't take his eyes off of Sister Mary's thighs. He was sitting there as if he was daydreaming about what he could do to her in the church's men's bathroom. She flirted back, licking her lips and fanning her breasts with the paper that held the printed agenda.

"Pay attention, you two," Daddy said as he caught the exchange. "I motion that Missy Rochelle Jones take over in the role of Pastor for Mt. Zion Holiness Church effective next Sunday."

"I second that motion," Deacon Freemon said as he gulped.

Mother Smithfield looked puzzled at the obvious exchanges, considering Sister Mary was engaged to be married. She called her on it, whispering, "You are a woman of God. Now don't you go lusting after the devil, you hear me?"

Sister Mary ignored her comments as she smacked her lips and continued to stare.

"May I say something?" I asked, still stunned by today's news.

"Sure, Missy," Daddy said with his hands crossing over each other.

"I know this is random, but I think we should have some Sundays where we have a praise and worship team come up and sing instead of always asking the choir for selections. If we are moving into the twenty-first century church, then we must begin to do twenty-first century things."

"I think that is a great idea, Pastor Elect Missy," Deacon Freemon said as his eyes bounced onto Michelle. Deacon Freemon was Natalia's father and an old playa who could not control his fetish for women. He glided into church each Sunday with his top hat and his multi-colored socks that matched his tie. He was too smooth not to be noticed and Sister Mary seemed willing to take a chance on Mr. Goodbar, in spite of her committed relationship. He tugged on his suspenders, giving lots of feedback on the new generation church. "Are we going to have a church theme like them T. D. Jakes and Creflo churches? You gonna do those week-long sermons and stuff?"

"That sounds like a great idea, Deacon. I think we are all on the right path with this." Mother Smithfield grinned as she wiggled her straw hat on her head.

"All right then, we have a plan. Let's not forget that Michelle will be our lead musician. I vote that Michelle Hanks take over the position as the lead musician and Tommy Lee Davis is dismissed effective immediately," Daddy said as he pointed in her direction.

"I second that motion," Deacon Freemon said, adjusting his tie. Everyone clapped and stood up for both favorable votes that were presented.

"Happy to have her back with us," Mother Smithfield said to Michelle.

"Well praise God!" Mother Gaines wiggled in her seat ready to dance.

Pastor looked over at Sister Mary hoping to get her back on track without calling her out. "You still getting married next month, gal?" he asked as he looked back and forth between the flirting.

"Oh, Yeah, right. The big day will be next month," she replied as she fanned her breasts once again, this time with her hands.

"We will make sure that the music is covered," Michelle said.

"Uh huh," she stammered as saliva began to formulate at the corner of her lips. It was as if everyone could see her hormones through her tight red dress as she sat staring into space.

"You all right, gal? You look like you saw Jesus," Pastor said sarcastically.

"Oh yes, I am doing fine," she sighed.

"Let's adjourn this meeting, I have things to do. I'm sure we all have things to do." Mother Smithfield looked over at me, smiling as if she knew my plans.

The meeting was adjourned. Each member hugged and shook hands on their way out the door. Daddy walked over to me and Michelle and asked, "You all feel good about this move?"

We exchanged looks and said, "Yes, we're good!"

" I guess the journey begins now, huh?"

I began to shuffle my feet like Mike Tyson before entering into the ring. "I am ready for the challenge, Daddy. I have a lot of unfinished business to handle before I take full control. I have some people to take care of."

"What do you mean by that, gal? Now don't go out there and do something stupid and get yourself locked up in the county jail," he said.

"I got this, Daddy." My eyes burned again, thinking about different ways to demolish the existence of Tommy Lee Davis and Olivia Wallace. "Let me take you home, Michelle; I'm sure Beanie will be here any minute now."

"I can't wait to meet the Jamaican boy. We got dinner after service on Sunday. Do you think he will eat some potato salad and collards?" Daddy looked, trying to figure out our foreign guest.

"He is from Jamaica, Daddy, not Australia. They do eat some of the same foods you know."

We looked at each other and giggled. "Daddy, he will have no problem eating what we eat."

"Thanks for everything, Pastor. I will be on the big Hammond organ bright and early Sunday morning," Michelle said.

"All right now. Lord have mercy, we are going to have a shouting time! Tell that Jamaican boy I said hello and I'll see you gals tomorrow so I can meet him."

We walked out the door and I said to Michelle, "You sure you're all right?"

"I am fine, chile. Don't worry about me."

"After I meet up with Beanie maybe we can all come together later at the church, so I can go over some songs with you tomorrow."

"That would be great. I don't want to mess the choir up not knowing the songs."

I nudged her arm. "You? Mess us up? You got jokes," I laughed loudly.

"Okay, what time should we meet?"

"Meet me around seven p.m."

"Sounds good. Let me take you home."

We walked in silence and I could only imagine how she was feeling. Lord have mercy on my soul. The sweetest girl I knew was now a woman scorned. Lord give her strength.

THAT CHURCH LIFE

Chapter 23

Friday evening, Beanie arrived in the state known for beer, barbecue and tobacco. I met him on the Avondale exit off of Hwy 85 South. He pulled up in a shiny blue Cadillac with factory rims and rolled right next to me. I ran up to the car as he stepped out, hugging him tightly.

He wore a casual jogging suit with matching sneakers and stood straight like a king who had found his queen. He put his hands around my waist and looked into my eyes. One thing was for sure, I wanted him to be with me forever. I felt safe. I felt secure. I felt loved.

"Hey, me lady?" he said in a soft voice.

I reached up to kiss his silky lips while pulling his neck closer to me. I paused. "I really missed you, sir. Are you hungry?"

"I guess I could eat a little."

"Follow me to my house so that we can park your car. I'll take you to my special restaurant, with the best catfish in town," I suggested. Hwy 85 South was our destination as we got off on the

Duke Street exit. He parked his car in the apartment complex lot and jumped into the Maxima without flinching.

"There is this great southern food restaurant that I think you will enjoy. After we eat, I have to go to the church and meet my friend, Michelle for a mini rehearsal session. Is that okay with you?"

"Wherever you go, I will follow, me lady." He patted me on my shoulder giving me a mini massage.

Making our way to the Famous Fish Hut Restaurant on Hwy 55 was the answer to all hunger woes. The big, fried crispy scallops with sea salt, fried haddock with white bread and stuffed mango shrimp could not be compared with any other restaurant in Durham. People drove from everywhere to eat there because it was common knowledge that they had the best fried fish in North Carolina. Arriving at the restaurant, the owner greeted us with southern hospitality.

"Howdy, how y'all doing tonight?"

"We're doing fine, Brother Joe, how about you?" I asked.

"I can't complain. It's been a good week here at the restaurant."

"I'm sure with all these homecoming customers coming into town."

"Yup, ain't nothing like homecoming time. What a cute couple." We looked at each bashfully. "What are you having today?"

"We will have two fried catfish sandwiches on white bread with lots of hot sauce!" I responded.

THAT CHURCH LIFE

Brother Joe took our order and said, "We have some lemon meringue pie that was made just an hour ago. Would you like to try some?"

Beanie looked up at him and said, "That sounds real good, mon."

"Where you from, son?" Brother Joe asked.

Showing his pearly whites, he said, "I'm from Ocho Rios, Jamaica, mon. Did my accent give me away?"

We all laughed, and Joe said, "Yeah, you ain't from around these parts talkin' like that, sir." He walked away and shouted, "Two catfish with two lemon pies. Extra hot sauce." He hit a silver bell that sat on the counter. We crossed arms and couldn't keep our hands off of each other. I was so glad to finally have him in my home town.

"I can't wait to show you around the city. I wish you had enough time here to participate in some of the activities in the area," I said while gazing into his eyes.

He stroked the palm of my hand. "This is my first of many visits. I can see me living here one day in the future."

"Is that so?" I asked as I grabbed his hands even tighter.

I looked out the restaurant window and noticed Natalia in the drive-through line waiting to order. "Oh wow, there's Natalia!"

He looked out the window and said, "Yes, I remember her well."

I waved to get her attention and after several minutes of jumping up and down she looked in my direction. She smiled as she got her food and parked her car. She ran inside to greet me.

"Hey, sis. Who are you here with?"

"I told you Beanie would be here this weekend." I pointed in his direction. "I thought you were out of town?"

"I just got back from a short flight assignment. I was actually going to surprise you at church tomorrow once I heard that Michelle would be on the organ."

"Now that's what's up!"

We continued to chat as Natalia came over and greeted Beanie. We laughed and joked for a while until our hot catfish sandwiches arrived on a small foam plate with a side of tartar sauce.

I bent my head down to take a bite of the savory catfish goodness when I heard someone call my name from behind.

"Missy, come here for a minute."

I looked up and it was Tommy, once again messing up the moment and causing havoc.

"I'm sorry, I'm eating right now. I don't have time to talk to you." I looked away and continued to eat.

Beanie paused, watching him carefully.

Tommy limped over to our table and stood in front of us while Natalia sat on the edge of the seat looking ready to bust a move.

"So, you gonna act like you don't hear me calling, huh?"

"I heard you and I said I can't talk to you right now."

He reached out his hand to Beanie and said, "Oh, you must be the dude on all her voicemails. What's up, partna? I'm Tommy."

Beanie ignored the handshake and responded, "Beanie is the name."

"Sounds like you got a little accent going on there, sir. Didn't know the little church girl messed around with foreigners."

Natalia and I exchanged looks as Beanie stood up from his seat.

"Look, man, we are trying to eat our food. Is there a problem here?"

"Nah, ain't no problem at all. Just wanted to say hello." He put his hand on my hair as Beanie grabbed his hand.

"I suggest you go back to where you came from, Limp-a-lot. You're disturbing our dinner."

Natalia jumped up and pushed Tommy out of the way. "Get out of here, dude, before we show you something!"

"It's cool. It's cool. I don't need any trouble here. See you later, baby."

I threw my sandwich down in the center of my plate and said, "Not your baby anymore, loser. Now get lost."

Tommy turned around and walked toward the front door. He threw up the peace sign and blew kisses from the window. His behavior didn't bother Beanie at all as he continued to eat his food and lick tartar sauce off his fingers.

"I see Mr. B don't flinch for punks," Natalia said, raising her fist high up in the air.

He scooped a teaspoonful of tartar sauce onto his sandwich and said, "I didn't come here to beef with her old boyfriends. I came to show her what her new man is about." He puckered his lips, waiting for me to meet halfway. I reached over to great him with kiss.

Natalia leaned her elbow on the table. "I like you already. She needs a strong man like you. But that's one dude you don't have to worry about. He only challenges women. I knew he wouldn't step to a real man."

"Enough. Hey, we're going by the church for rehearsal. Since you're off, do you want to chill with us?"

"I was going by the church anyway. I talked to Michelle this morning and she said she would tighten up my weave right after rehearsal. So I told her I would come up to the church to hear her play."

"What a pleasant surprise." I wiped my mouth, as grease landed around it and my lower cheeks.

"That's a weave? That must be that expensive straight hair the ladies buy all the time," he asked as he examined her head. "Glad you're here, Ms. Talia. This is what I like to see. Loving and caring friends around me lady."

"Yeah, my circle is limited. I don't mess around with too many females anyway."

"That's a good thing," he said, taking another bite of his food.

THAT CHURCH LIFE

We finished eating and headed out toward the church. Natalia followed behind us while stuffing the rest of her food down in the car.

We entered the church being our playful selves as Michelle sat on the organ, waiting for our arrival.

"Looks like the gang's all here." Michelle looked up and greeted us. "We've got to get these notes down pat for tomorrow. I can't wait!"

We practiced two songs as Beanie and Natalia joined in from the front pew. We completed the last and final note and gave each other a high five.

"Michelle already has this information but for Natalia and Beanie, I have been designated as the new pastor of the church starting next Sunday." I jumped up and down clapping my hands.

"You mean to tell me you held that info until now?" Natalia said as she came over to hug me tightly around my neck. "That is awesome, sis!"

Beanie twirled me around in a circle as if we were Julie Andrews and Christopher Plummer in *The Sound of Music*.

"Let me show you my new office, people. You're gonna love it! I made major changes."

The crew followed me to the study when we heard the back door slam. Daddy came in unexpectedly and heard our voices.

"Well, well, well. The church girl crew, plus one, are in the house of God. How y'all doing on this fine and wonderful rain-free evening?"

"Dad, this is Beanie. Beanie, this is my father, Pastor Henry Jenkins!"

"A pleasure to meet you, sir," he said as he shook his hand. "You have one lovely daughter."

"Ahh, a gentleman, huh? I like you already, Jamaican boy. Come here and give me a hug! Welcome to the family!"

Beanie grinned at Daddy's southern drawl as we all walked to the office. We opened the door wide as everyone stepped in to analyze all of the changes I'd made by adding a feminine touch.

"Lawd, you called in the painters that quick and got someone to fix this up? It's only been a few days. Now this definitely looks like your style. Proud of you, gal."

I smiled and said, "Yes, they did a great job. I'm not finished adding my own personalized touch to it but I should be finished by next week."

I replaced the gray and dingy curtains with purple sheer laced ones. I grouped all family pictures on the book shelf along with photos of myself in my preaching robe. We were all talking at once about the purple décor and the additional lamps added when we heard another slam of the back door.

"Are you all expecting anyone else?" Daddy asked, looking around.

"No, we didn't tell anyone else about our meeting, Daddy."

"Lord, I don't have time to deal with Olivia right now. Jesus help us," Daddy said opening the door to check around as a bat swung high in the air, hitting him right in the center of his head. The sudden blunt force knocked him down to the floor instantly. We all looked up with our mouths wide open.

"What in the world?" I yelled as I rushed toward Daddy for assistance.

Tommy Lee Davis stood in front of my father and yanked my arm as I reached down checking Daddy's condition.

"I told you, you would never find another like me. Did you think I was just going to let you go that easily? Huh?" he said as he yanked me harder toward him. He pulled me away from the others, backing out of the office.

"Oh my God!" screamed Natalia. "What is wrong with you? Why must you continue to bring this woman grief like this? Leave her alone!"

Michelle's screams drowned out Tommy's explanation as to why he was taking me with him. Natalia and Beanie rushed to the door with their hands reaching out trying to help me.

"If you don't let her go, today will be the last day of your life. I told Missy, he is plum crazy!" Natalia stepped closer. The closer she came to him, the more he stepped back, jerking me from side to side.

"Step back or we are going to have some problems!"

"Let her go!" Natalia said.

Tommy pushed me to his left hip and pulled out a knife. The instrument was so long it could slice a watermelon with one try.

"What's up now, Jamaican boy? You think you got a good one, huh?"

"Eh, mon, please let her go. Don't do this. Let us help you."

"Get back on the plane and leave her here with me. That's how you can help." The knife moved closer to my neck as he continued to talk. He began to sob as his face wrinkled. Tears dripped on to my blouse as he repositioned his hold and now held me in a headlock. "She is all I got, man. No one has loved me like she has... I can't let you or anyone else have her."

Michelle rocked back and forth, looking suicidal. "Let her go you, maniac! Haven't you hurt enough people and caused enough damage?"

He looked at Michelle with sorrowful eyes. "You didn't tell her, did you?"

Michelle stood up with her head held high, answering, "Yes, she knows everything you did to me, everything, rapist!" Michelle picked up the vase sitting on the end of the desk and threw it with full force. He ducked as he dropped the knife to the floor.

This was the opportunity to break free. I took my shoulder and shoved it back into his chest. He fell on the other side of Daddy's unresponsive body. Beanie, Michelle and Natalia rushed him as we all tussled to the floor. Beanie jumped on his back holding onto him as if he was riding a horse. Natalia reached for the knife, but it dropped again. Beanie struggled and rolled around on the floor with everyone trying to pull them apart. Michelle continued to scream, as she and Natalia tried to grab me. I struggled to get away as Beanie continued to pull him off of me from behind. We tried to get up but then we all fell onto the floor in a pile of bodies. We rolled closer to the window. The curtain came down with us as Tommy's feet were tangled by the sheer chiffon. I didn't know who had the knife but I knew it was somewhere beneath the pile. That was when Tommy cried out in pain and let me go. Beanie jumped up and grabbed me and pulled me away from Tommy who was clutching his stomach. When I stood up, I had blood on my clothes and hands.

Déjà vu! It's all happening again! Beanie's hands were also covered in blood. Natalia scrambled to get up off the floor as Daddy's eyes flittered for help. "I'm bleeding." Tommy looked down at his hands that were covered with blood from several stab wounds in his stomach. "Who did this? Who cut me?"

Tommy struggled to stand up, then reached for the other curtain to steady himself. But he fell again as he yanked the curtain from the window. The curtain covered his body.

Everyone stood there watching as blood seeped into the curtain. We looked at each other in shock, trying to comprehend what just happened until we realized that Tommy wasn't moving.

"Is he dead?" Natalia asked as she peeked down, tilting her head to the side.

"I don't know! Oh my God!" I said.

Scared and confused, I started screaming. "Oh my God! Oh my God, what have we done?"

"Calm down, Missy, it's going to be okay," Beanie said. He pulled the curtain off Tommy and he counted the cuts on his body. "There're eighteen cuts. How did this happen? Who had the knife?" Beanie asked, checking to see if Tommy was breathing.

"His life doesn't matter at all to me right now. What matters is you're safe and free and that bastard is finally dead!" Michelle yelled.

"No, no, no, this can't be happening," I cried.

THAT CHURCH LIFE

Chapter 24

We all stood over Tommy still in shock. He didn't have a pulse; he laid limp and lifeless. Michelle could not stop crying as she moved to the corner of the room with her legs up and her arms over them, rocking in slow motion. Natalia stood with her arms folded looking down at him with a blank stare. Daddy sat up straight holding his head and looked straight across at the bloody curtain.

"My head hurts so badly. What did I get hit with?"

"He hit you with a bat, Pastor. Knocked you out cold," Natalia responded.

"Is he dead?" he asked.

Natalia responded with a cold expression. "I sure as hell hope so."

I went over to comfort Michelle as she continued to rock.

"It will be all right, everyone. It was self-defense," Beanie added.

Unfortunately, in the state of North Carolina, she could still be charged even if it looked like self-defense.

Michelle stood up, even though she was still rocking back and forth. "It's okay, honey, he's dead. You're free, sis, you're free. We are all free!"

She looked at me and put her face on my chest. "What are we going to do, Missy? What are we going to do?"

"It will be all right hun. We will live, that's what we'll do." I rocked her like a baby trying to get her back to reality. It was as if she had seen a ghost.

Beanie and Natalia looked at each other. Beanie said, "So, do we want to call the police or do we want to hide the body?"

Everyone turned to him and said in unison, "Hide the body?"

Daddy chuckled. "Boy, we don't do that over here in America. We can't just bury folks anywhere we want, you know."

"I was just trying to help. I guess I don't need to elaborate on my past," Beanie said.

Natalia shook her head. "Yeah, now might not be a good time for that. Let's just call the police and tell them it was self-defense. But who had the knife?"

Michelle collapsed, leaning on the wall.

"I guess that answers your question, huh?" I said as I looked down at her curled feet. "It's going to be okay, Michelle. We have your back."

Beanie dialed 911 on his cell phone. "Hello, we had an intruder enter our church. Please come to…" He looked around waiting for us to tell him the address. "Four fifty-three RTP Parkway, Mt. Zion

Holiness Church in Durham. Hurry! We think the intruder might be expired."

Thirty minutes later, the ambulance, police team and Channel 5 news arrived on the scene. We stood outside as they tore my newly furnished office into a million pieces. Beanie rubbed my back, not worried at all, while everyone else hugged up on one another for comfort.

"It's going to be all right, children. God is going to see us through this. He always does," Daddy said.

I looked over, giving him a huge smile. I was somewhat relieved that this was all behind us now and I could move on with my life.

As we continued to stand outside, the church phone wouldn't stop ringing.

"Who keeps calling?" Daddy asked.

I stepped inside the hallway to answer. "It must be urgent." I picked the phone up and said, "Hello."

"Hello, is this Missy?"

"Yes."

The caller had a maniacal laugh. "You thought you could get rid of me, huh? You thought that if your daddy gave you his title that I would go away."

I knew who it was but I was hoping that it was all a dream. "I'm sorry, who is this?"

"Your worst nightmare."

I paused. "Olivia?"

"The one and only. I came to the church looking for your daddy again and guess what I have on tape?" She paused and laughed loudly. "I have you and all your friends committing a murder. I got you now and there is nothing you can do about it."

My eyes rose in terror wondering how in the world Olivia even got a glimpse of what just happened. I began to think about the curtains being pulled and Michelle stabbing him underneath the pile eighteen times.

I screamed, "I hate you! It was self-defense! And who said he was dead?" I clutched my chest and bent over thinking about what she would do to us.

"That boy got to be dead after what I just watched. Now give me my money, church girl!"

The dial tone rang loud in my ear as I stood still and trembled. I couldn't imagine the trouble Michelle would be in if the video didn't look like a self-defense case.

"Lord, what do we do now?"

To be continued…

THAT CHURCH LIFE

ABOUT THE AUTHOR

Teresa B. Howell was raised in Boston, Massachusetts. She is an educator, mentor and advocate for students with special needs. Born and raised in the church, it was fitting to tell her story. She currently resides in Durham, NC with her husband and children.

That Church Life! is available on Amazon.com and Barnesandnoble.com. Visit www.teresabhowell.com to order or for updates and events.

Made in the USA
Middletown, DE
15 June 2019